A MARRIAGE MADE IN MAYFAIR

Scandalous London Series

TAMARA GILL

D0111119

A Marriage Made in Mayfair
Scandalous London Series
Novella Three

Copyright 2015 by Tamara Gill
Cover Art by EDH Graphics

ISBN-13: 9781973267706

DEDICATION

For my forever tolerant family.
I love you guys.
Xxxx

CHAPTER 1

"Are you sure you want to do this, Suzanna?" asked Henry, as he watched her preparations from the doorway.

"Of course. I'm sure. Lord Danning may have frightened me off last season, but he'll not do it again." She shifted her gaze away from her brother as her French maid Celeste pinned a curl to dangle alluringly over her ear.

Henry pushed himself away from the doorframe and strolled over to where she sat in front of her dressing table. He held out his hand and pulled Suzanna to her feet, twirling her slowly as he admired her. "Well, you'll certainly turn heads at the ball. Celeste has worked miracles. I hardly recognize my clumsy, unfashionable little sister."

Suzanna glanced at her reflection—nothing about this sophisticated woman staring back at her resembled the humiliated, heartbroken debutante who ran, not only from a ballroom, but also from the country.

Gone were the orange locks that had hung with no life about her shoulders and the eyebrows that were forever in need of plucking. Even the little mole above her lip looked delicate and not at all unattractive, as some matrons had once pointed out.

Oh yes, she would draw attention tonight, but if truth be told, there was only one head she really wanted to turn.

"You like this new look, Mademoiselle March?" asked Celeste.

Her eyes sparkled with expectation. "I do." She laughed. "Oh, Celeste, thank you so very much. You have outdone yourself."

And Royce Durnham, Viscount Danning, could grovel at her silk slippers for all she cared. A grin quirked her lips over the thought of seeing one of London's most powerful men clasping her skirts, tears welling in his eyes begging for forgiveness. It would only serve him right, especially after the atrocious set-down bestowed on her last year at her coming out.

Celeste clucked in admonishment. "My profession is so much easier when one has so beautiful a canvas with which to work. I only make improvement with what is before me."

"Too true," Henry stated, kissing his sister's cheek.

Suzanna laughed. Perhaps they were right. For it was *she* who stared back with green eyes so large they seemed to pale the freckles across her nose to insignificance. "I can only hope my deportment has also improved. I was such a calamity last season."

"Was your first season, *oui*?"

"Yes." Suzanna walked over to the window and looked out onto the grounds of her father's London townhouse. "Father having made his money in trade ensured my lack of popularity. I was certainly not fit for some of the mamas of the *ton*." She shrugged away the stinging memory of their rejection. The worst had come from the lofty Lord

Danning, a rich, powerful aristocrat, tall with an athletic frame that bespoke of hours in the saddle. He was a gentleman who always dressed in immaculate attire that fitted his body like a kid leather glove, but without the airs of a dandy.

Even the memory of a strong jaw and dark-blue eyes made her belly clench with longing. He was the embodiment of everything one looked for in a husband—until he opened his mouth, spoke, and ruined all such musings.

"Your father was knighted, mademoiselle. Surely, the English aristocracy would not slight your family's humble beginnings. Everyone must start somewhere. *No?*"

"You are right, Celeste, yet perhaps if it had been a more distant relation than my father who made our fortune, the *ton* may have been more favourable toward me. No matter my obscene dowry, they did not welcome me as warmly as some of the other girls."

Henry growled his disapproval. "I'll meet you downstairs, Suzanna, before my temper is unleashed on the *ton's* ideals. Aunt Agnes will be down soon to accompany us, so do not delay." He marched from the room.

"I'll be down shortly." Suzanna sat at her desk and picked up her quill, idly rolling it between her fingers. She was glad she had thought to write to Victoria. Her dearest and best friend would ensure she arrived tonight at the Danning's ball in the company of friends.

"I'll wear the light green silk tonight, Celeste," she said, placing the quill onto the desk. "And Mary," she said to her second maid who fluttered about, tidying the room. "Could you bring my supper up to my bedchamber straightaway? I don't have much time to get ready."

Her maid curtsied and departed. Celeste pulled her gown from the armoire. "There is a small wrinkle, mademoiselle. I will take it downstairs and quickly press it. Your hair and lips, I will repair when you have finished the supper. *Oui?*"

Suzanna smiled. "Thank you. I must admit to being a little excited about going. It has been months since I was in London, and the ball is supposed to be the event of the season."

"And you, mademoiselle, will be the most beautiful of all!"

Suzanna chuckled as the door closed behind her servant. The most beautiful; well, perhaps this once. Maybe if she acted with all the decorum and manners hammered into her over the last few months, a man might magically fall at her feet with an offer of marriage. At one and twenty, marriage was certainly what one ought to think on. Just not with Lord Danning. Not any more, at least.

Hateful cad.

CHAPTER 2

"Lord Danning, allow me to explain once more. The cost of running your thoroughbred breeding programme, the living expenses on your estates here in England and Italy, along with your excessive lifestyle, are leaving you very short on funds.

"I'm sorry to be the one to tell you such unwelcome news, but the extreme way of life you and your brother—whom you fund—live, has finally taken a toll. You have three months at most to settle the debts of your family, or I'm afraid you are facing debtors' prison."

Royce swore and slumped back in his chair. He glanced up at the harsh, no-nonsense visage of his solicitor, Mr. Andrews, and cringed. He had expected this meeting would not be to his liking. But such news as his ruination was not quite what he'd imagined.

"Can I not sell off more of my estate?"

"What remains of the property is entailed for future generations. You have already sold off what you could. Furnishings, material objects will only buy you weeks at the most. Of course, any *family* pieces must remain with the estate." Mr. Andrews paused. "Perhaps you could sell off the hunters and some equipages, my lord? Or the property in Rome?"

Royce halted the drumming of his fingers against the table. "You mock me, sir? Broke I may be, but I'm still a lord with friends in high places. These same friends who would be willing to cease using your services should I tell them you have lost your senses. Sell off my carriages and horseflesh. Whoever heard of such a preposterous idea?"

"Apologies, my lord, but again, I must speak frankly. As your financial counsellor, I must advise closing down the London home, or better yet, renting it out for the season and returning to your country estate."

"What?" Royce asked, his voice harder than it ought to be against the man. Mr. Andrews was only doing his job after all. He gritted his teeth, calming his ire.

"For months, my lord, I cautioned you, warned you this would occur, and yet you ignored me. You must rein in the excessive expenditures your family can no longer afford. Your name is an asset in the *ton*; use it, and procure a rich wife. My apologies for speaking out of turn."

"You think you're the only one who is displeased? I'm a Danning, proud of my lineage, and the blood of the great men that flows through my veins. A family line handed down unblemished from father to son. And now, I, the current viscount, protector of my family, could lose it all."

Royce stood and strode over to the decanter of brandy. His hands shook as he poured the fiery liquid. The burning sting of the drink warmed his belly, yet his body remained cold.

"What do I do?" The life he lived could not be over. To lose one's station in life was beyond imagining. He could not be...poor! The thought of debtor's prison, where lice and fleas were as common as a cellmate, sent a shiver of revulsion down his spine.

"As I said, marry an heiress. And be quick about it, mind."

Royce placed his second glass of brandy upon the sideboard and frowned. "I had not thought of such a possibility." His solicitor threw him a sceptical look. "Well, of course I've thought of marriage, just not marriage to a wealthy woman. We Dannings have always been comfortable with our financial position; marrying for money has never been a priority for me." Royce paused in thought. "Certainly it would allow the family to continue to live on as before." His solicitor made a choking sound, his plump chin meeting his chest in disapproval. "You wish to say something further, Mr. Andrews."

"Your family cannot continue spending, my lord. The income you procure from your estate is not enough to cover your expenditures with your horses, let alone season after season of spending as if money is no object. Your investment income from the East India Company has yet to arrive and may not for many months. You make no money, my lord. Certainly not enough to keep you in the current lifestyle you lead. Your brother especially cannot continue with his life as it is now. He exceeds his monthly income tenfold, which you pay whenever a debtor knocks on your door."

Mr. Andrews cleared his throat and met his gaze squarely. "If you wish to secure the well-being of your future children, limitations must be put in place and adhered to."

Royce bowed his head. The old solicitor was right. His brother would have to be brought to heel, and along with it his own expenditures.

"Right, then. I'm sure I can bring order to the family's

troubles...and my brother," he said, forming a plan in his mind. "Well, I'd best be preparing for the ball."

"A ball, my lord? Excuse me for speaking out again, but you cannot possibly afford to throw a ball. If I may make another suggestion—best you procure an Almack's voucher, and make an appearance at the patroness's expense," Mr. Andrews said, bending down to place his papers into his leather carry bag.

"Mr. Andrews, you are well aware I throw the ball of the season every year. One no one would miss. Why, have you not noticed my staff bustling about, busy with the preparations?" Royce strode toward the door. "I'm sure, though as my new financial situation is not yet known, there will be many a young filly entering my door, eager to marry a viscount. I shall simply favour only those of sufficient wealth."

"Sounds like a marriage made in heaven, my lord."

"No." Royce grinned. "A marriage made in Mayfair."

With a curt nod, his solicitor slapped on his hat, tapped the top, and left.

Royce leaped up the stairs and sauntered toward his living quarters. The old codger had finally proved worthy. The idea of courting an heiress was just what he needed. Perhaps his brother would follow suit and marry one as well. Then at least George wouldn't be pulling on his coat tails every week for more coin.

The thought of never being plump in the pocket again sent a shiver of revulsion down his spine. All the Dannings before him, generations of wealthy English lords, would rise up from their graves in protest should he fail to marry well and lose his estate.

Well, he wouldn't allow such a thing.

He would find a woman, marry her, and ensure that his family's future was secure.

Royce pulled at his cravat and rang for his valet, his thoughts absorbed with the guests due to arrive at his home for the ball tonight.

Those of the highest peerage with money enough to please the monarchy would attend. Surely a wife could be found amongst the pretty women who will undoubtedly fall at his feet.

Begging to be his countess and wife.

CHAPTER 3

Suzanna nodded her thanks as she passed a flute of champagne to her friend. The ball was a crush, full to the brim with the *ton's* highest patrons, many of whom looked down their noses at the young heiress.

"It's extremely warm in here tonight," Victoria said, fanning herself with a silk fan that matched her dress. "I believe I may have to walk the terrace soon, or I'm certain I may faint."

"Do you intend to walk out there alone?" Suzanna laughed at the crimson blush that stole over her friend's cheeks.

"No, I'll have you by my side." She gestured toward the card room door not far from where they stood. "I see Viscount Danning is extremely dashing this eve. Never have I seen such a fine piece of masculinity within the *ton*, and so attentive to the ladies, if I may say so."

Suzanna gazed over at the man she had followed like a ninny hammer last season. She threw him a baleful glare she hoped pricked his senses and hurt every fiber of his being. Not that he was looking her way, of course. Seemed nothing had changed in the year she'd been away. Being from trade, as she was deemed, wasn't of course worth admiring. "Yes." Suzanna took a sip of her drink. "He seems as stiff and as cold as ever."

Victoria chuckled. "Oh, I don't know. I think he seems...kind of sad tonight as if he's lost his best friend, or some such."

"I didn't know Lord Danning was capable of having a best friend."

"Oh, Suzanna, you are too cruel."

Something in her friend's tone made her senses bristle. "I didn't know you cared a fig what Lord Danning felt." She turned and looked at her.

Victoria blushed an even darker shade of crimson and waved her remark aside. "No, of course I do not. He is nothing to me. I was merely making a general observation."

Suzanna turned her gaze back to his lordship and wondered what had caused this sullen frown on his normally attractive features.

"And anyway, to term Lord Danning as cold and stiff is a little cruel. From memory I believe you named him the epitome of gentlemanly behaviour last season."

Suzanna inwardly cringed at the reminder. "I may have had such a ridiculous notion last year, but my thoughts are much altered this season, as you well know. I certainly do not think him so now."

Victoria touched her arm in a comforting gesture before her eyes widened and sparkled with joviality as she spied someone over Suzanna's shoulder. "Oh, here comes your brother. Do I appear well enough?"

"You are as beautiful as always," Suzanna said, as she turned toward her elder sibling.

With a sweeping bow, Henry took Victoria's hand then

kissed his sister's cheek. "May I say how beautiful you both look this eve, Suz, Lady Victoria." Her brother's gaze settled on Victoria with a twinkle in his dark green orbs.

She tittered, and Suzanna wondered when her brother would get up the courage to ask her dearest friend to marry him. Assuming she would be allowed to marry into gentry, one generation away from trade. Victoria, after all, was an earl's daughter.

"What brings you to our side, Henry? Come to sweep your wallflower sister from her seat and dance with her?"

"Of course I will dance with you, after I escort the delightful Lady Victoria out for the next set."

"I would like that very much, Mr. March," Victoria smiled, dazzling her brother once again.

Henry threw an exultant smile over his shoulder as they walked away. Alone, Suzanna sipped her drink and watched the dancers twirl and laugh on the ballroom floor. Many of the gentlemen here tonight had looked her way, but were yet to venture to her side. She checked her gown and touched her hair, making sure she didn't have anything out of place. Her Aunt Agnes smiled and waved from her situation, not a few seats away.

Suzanna smiled back and hoped she didn't disappoint her aunt with another disastrous season. Henry and she owed everything to their father's only living sister. After the tragic death of their parents in a carriage accident, Aunt Agnes had come to live with them and raised them as best she could.

Suzanna supposed her awkwardness in the *ton* could be due to the fact their aunt had grown up the daughter of a farmer and had never ventured into society. Not until Suzanna's father had made the sound investment in mining did the family start to move in different circles than those to which they were accustomed.

She looked at her Aunt Agnes and a lump formed in her throat. Her aunt also sat alone, preferring to speak little lest she say something that would cause strife for her charge. Love for the woman surged through Suzanna, and she promised herself this season would be different.

The humiliating memory of the Coots ball, when she'd walked from the retiring room with her gown askew, and showing enough ankle to make her red hair pale in comparison to her complexion, made her inwardly cringe.

What a horror last year's season was, certainly one to forget, and never to repeat. Surely after many months of learning to be a lady of the highest calibre she could manage to dance with someone other than her brother, and make her aunt happy.

"Good evening, Miss March."

Anyone, but him.

Suzanna swallowed a sip of champagne and watched Lord Danning bow, his dark, amused gaze looking up at her before he straightened. Her own narrowed.

"Evening, Lord Danning." *And I'm not at all in favour of speaking to you, you obnoxious rake, so please go away!*

"I hope you are well this eve, Miss March, and enjoying the ball?"

Suzanna barely stopped herself from rolling her eyes in disinterest at his contrived conversation. "I was enjoying it very well, my lord." *Until a minute or so ago.*

Lord Danning's lips twitched as if he understood her meaning. "I heard you travelled abroad over the past year?"

Suzanna pulled at the hem of her glove and met his lordship's gaze. "Yes, to Paris."

"You are much changed since I saw you last." His lordship handed her a glass of champagne and took her empty one without hesitation.

"I suppose you mean I'm no longer dressed like a disaster and my hair actually meets current fashion requirements."

He coughed. "I beg your pardon. Have I said something wrong, Miss March?"

Suzanna glanced at his immaculate attire with loathing. Damn the man to look perfect in every way. With very little effort, he always seemed able to appear pristine and relaxed. Yet Suzanna had to hire a French maid and take endless classes on deportment just so she could appear half respectable in society. She gritted her teeth at the vexing thought.

"I'm sorry, my lord, but I cannot understand why you are here talking to me. All you wished to say was more than adequately said last season, if I recall."

The colour drained from Lord Danning's face, leaving him a pasty shade of white. "Forgive me, Miss March. I was merely being polite. This is my ball, if you recall, and I do try to keep up with my duties as the host."

Suzanna smiled with no warmth behind the gesture. "Oh, I'm sure you were, my lord, but where your manners are concerned I care not."

His mouth gaped, reminding her of a fish. "You're angry with me." Lord Danning paused, his gaze speculative. "Why?"

"Why!" Suzanna shook her head at his question. Obviously, she was so unremarkable that their conversation in this very ballroom last year had been forgotten. "Perhaps you should seek out those who desire your company. I am not one of them."

He steered her behind a potted palm and hid her from the watchful eyes of the *ton*. Suzanna strove to calm her beating heart as the man she had longed for, wanted to kiss just once only months before, stared down at her with an emotion she could not place.

"You have changed not only your looks, Miss March. You seem to have procured a hatred for me while in Paris along with an uncommonly rude mouth."

Suzanna shut her gaping, *rude* mouth with a snap. "Rude, my lord? It is not I who is being rude. A gentleman who indicates he finds a woman's inner strength of character repulsive is the one being rude. Why don't you just admit you do not care for a woman who does not swoon at your feet, pining for a proposal of marriage?"

"I may have stated your mouth was uncommonly rude, but I did not say I found it repulsive, Miss March. If you would care to accompany me out to the terrace, I could show you just how non-repulsive I find your person."

Suzanna's feet, with a will of their own, stepped toward the terrace doors. Had she not wanted to have such a tryst with him last season? To kiss Lord Danning would be a dream come true. Heat stole up her neck at the resounding chuckle behind her before footfalls followed close on her heels.

The cool night air was a welcome balm when she stepped free of the ballroom crush. Strong fingers clasped her upper arm and pulled her toward a darkened stretch of the terrace.

An inner voice screamed at her to break free from his grasp and flee. Run as fast as she could from this bounder. But she would not. She would show the high and mighty Lord Danning what he had turned down and walked away from without a second thought. Tonight, it would be her opportunity to do the walking away. Excitement thrummed through her like a drug at the thought of her revenge, shallow as it was.

"You are very beautiful tonight," he said, coaxing her to sit on a stone seat hidden within an ivy-clad alcove.

"I do not need your praise, my lord. If you're going to kiss me, it would be wise to do so now before I return to the ballroom." Suzanna stiffened her spine and met his smiling gaze. He wouldn't be laughing for long.

"Last season, when I first saw you, ribbons and frills flying about you, I could not take my eyes from you."

Suzanna smiled and ran her hands up the lapels of his coat and noted the darkening of his eyes. "Because of the fright I made?"

"No." His attention fastened on her lips before slipping lower and admiring her person. "Because I saw the woman beneath all that decoration and knew I wanted her."

Suzanna ground her teeth, and raised his chin with one finger to bring his eyes back level to hers. "Why is it I find such words false, Lord Danning? Your actions and words last season spoke otherwise," she said in an accusing tone.

He shushed her and shifted her finger from his chin to his lips. Heat stole into her belly as his sinful lips kissed the tip of her finger, and her argument was lost to flame. Never had she experienced such a thing with a man, and as dreadfully wicked such a thought was, Suzanna couldn't help but wish for more of the same.

"They are the truth, whether you choose to believe them or not."

"Perhaps, my lord," she said, as she reclaimed her hand from his. "It is because you termed me from trade last season and not someone you wished to associate with, even as a friend."

How the memory of his hateful words hurt still. She beat back the urge to run, to get as far from this rogue as she could. To go to a place he could never hurt her with his lofty airs and opinions.

Never would she allow anyone to belittle her as he had, no matter their rank. Anger over the memory spiked her lust, and revenge simmered to a boil within her.

Lord Danning would pay.

Without hesitation, his lordship skimmed his lips against her throat, eliciting a sigh from Suzanna. Butterflies took flight in her belly, and her toes curled in her silk slippers.

"I do not recall mentioning your father's business dealings, Miss March. Are you certain I spoke so reprehensibly to you?"

"Yes," she said on a sigh, before clearing her throat. "Yes," she repeated, more strongly. "You did. And if they were not your exact words, it was what you implied."

"What am I implying now?"

Suzanna swallowed a moan and took her bottom lip between her teeth when his tongue slid up her neck, and he gently nibbled on her earlobe. *Oh dear, she should stop him now before they went any further, perhaps this kiss was a bad idea after all.* Her fingers curled about his lapels, pulling him closer. Lavender soap permeated the air along with a smell that was wholly Lord Danning, intoxicating and all male.

"You have the most exquisite skin, Miss March," he said, shifting closer and turning her toward him.

Suzanna's mouth dried when his hand clasped her hip, the silk of her gown no impediment to his ardent touch. His grasp slid downward to span her thigh where he lifted her leg slightly to sit higher against his own. It left her feeling open and vulnerable, and wholly excited.

Damn him.

"I want to kiss every inch of your skin."

A flush of heat rose under her gown with the thought. "I hope you are not planning to do such a thing here, my lord."

"No." He chuckled. "But perhaps we may find another secluded alcove where you will grant me such favours."

Suzanna shook her head. "I do not think so, my lord."

"Just a kiss then?" He pulled back and stared at her a moment. His gaze glistened with challenge in the dim light.

Suzanna chuckled. The laughing, teasing man before her reminded her of the Lord Danning she thought she knew and proclaimed a friend last season before his atrocious behaviour. Feelings she squashed rose within her, and so too, a pang of sadness; that although she would welcome his kiss, wished it in fact, she was not as fond of Lord Danning as one ought to be at such a moment. She could not quell her need to teach the high stickler a lesson he'd never forget in manners and in how to treat a lady.

"Just a kiss," she said.

It was far from just a kiss…

When his lips touched hers, Suzanna lost all memory of his slight, the harsh words spoken between them and her revenge. Gone was the lady who spent hours on deportment, hair, fashion, speech and anything else you could think of to be a diamond of the *ton*. In her place sat a woman who wanted the touch of a man. And not just any man, but Lord Danning.

The one man she no longer even liked.

CHAPTER 4

R oyce clasped Suzanna's jaw and let his fingers slide
into her hair. She was so altered since last year—
lusciously thick strands of golden-red curls, now expertly
coiffured to accentuate the greenest, brightest eyes he'd
ever seen. He had noticed her immediately at her coming
out ball. Fresh from the country, the woman had been
awkward and unsure of herself, with no idea of her beauty.
But her beauty was no longer hidden. Innocent longing,
unlike any he'd ever known stared up at him and left him
breathless.

His lips touched hers, and he was lost.

Royce allowed himself to be swept away into the
firestorm of desire burning through his body. Never had
soft lips and a tentative tongue excited him as much as it
did now. He pulled her hard against him, and immediately,
the intoxicating scent of jasmine enthralled him. Her
ardent response to his kiss urged him to take the intimate
interlude to a more satisfying conclusion, but the
gentleman within him urged caution.

After his mistreatment of her last season, Suzanna

deserved more than a rough tumble in the vine. For all her untutored yet delicious kiss, she was untouched. Royce didn't yet know if she was a candidate for his future wife, but what he did understand was to gain her with such underhanded scandalous means would not be favourable to an agreeable or pleasurable future. And after his first, enthralling taste of her lips, he decided if they were to have a future together it would be a pleasurable one, not one founded on regret and shame.

He tilted her chin and deepened the kiss, leaving no doubt as to the effect she had on him. The touch of her fingers, delightful and tentative, made him burn. He throbbed, wanted to lift her skirts and have her up against the ivy-covered trellis. Have her moan his name against his ear as her hot core clamped around him, draining him of his own release.

Royce pulled away, shocked at his own reactions and dishonourable thoughts about the woman. She stared up at him with glassy, lust-fogged eyes that gleamed in the dappled moonlight. "You should return to the ball before you're missed," he said.

Her pink tongue slipped out onto her bottom lip as if to tease him completely senseless. Stifling a growl, Royce stood and lifted her to her slippered feet, then set about removing the telling evidence she had been thoroughly kissed and manhandled by a rogue.

With gentle precision, he positioned a misplaced curl back within the bonds of a pin, the soft curl tempting him to bury his hands in her silken locks. She would look exquisite with her golden-red hair cascading about her shoulders. Or better yet, against his pillows, all mussed from his lovemaking.

She slapped his hand away and stepped back. "I am perfectly able to right my dress and appearance, my lord."

"Of course, Miss March," he said unable to hide the smile in his voice.

"I suppose a gentleman of your reputation thinks of such trysts as normal and commonplace, certainly something to laugh about."

"On the contrary, Miss March, and if I have offended you, please accept my most humble apologies." Royce bit back a smile. She was a delightful minx to behold, feathers ruffled and indignant. A twinge pricked in his chest and he frowned.

She curtsied. "Good night, Lord Danning."

Royce clasped her fingers before she could stalk away and didn't miss the slight tremble that thrummed against his palm. "Good night, Miss March." The urge to kiss her again nearly overrode his control, but the defiant gleam in her eye told him she'd not take well to more kisses from him this eve, even upon her hand.

Still, plenty of other eves in the season.

Royce watched her walk toward the terrace doors, her skirts billowing about long, striding legs, leaving him in the shadows with desires that ran as hot as the Arabian desert during the midday sun. Miss March had always been delectable. Now, she was desirable.

છૐ

Later that night, Royce watched Suzanna waltz gracefully with Lord Moyle and a simmering anger he thought never to feel started to burn in his gut. Grudgingly, he acknowledged the nuance for what it was. Jealousy.

"May I grant you my heartfelt condolences, Lord Danning?"

Royce beat back the urge to snarl at Suzanna's brother.

"What do you mean, March?" He took a swig of his brandy, welcoming the distraction of the burn from his growing temper. How dare this bastard speak to him after the trouble he'd caused with his own fool of a sibling.

"As I understand it, you will soon be married." March smirked and looked out over the gathered throng of guests.

Royce frowned. "So the banns have been read? Comical. I hadn't thought I'd asked a woman to be my bride." He clenched his jaw at the resounding chuckle, which grated on his already frayed nerves.

"Well of course you will, my lord. A ruined viscount must marry, and soon. I should imagine you have your sights set on someone…wealthy?"

Equal to his own height, Royce glared into March's eyes, one burning question fogging his mind: how had the bastard found out his situation was so desperate? "Not unlike yourself, a grandson of a farmer trying to marry an earl's daughter. Do not think yourself so much different, March. At least I have no need to climb the social ladder, only to keep what is rightfully mine from birth." Royce inwardly cringed as Suzanna's words stabbed at his conscience. Perhaps he was too high in the instep.

March paused. "*Touché*. And you may do whatever you wish as long as the woman you seek is not my sister."

With a will of their own, Royce's gaze sought out the beautiful Miss March. She shone like the brightest candle flame in a room full of superbly gowned women. A rare light and one to be treasured.

Suzanna laughed at something Lord Moyle said, and a pang of regret pierced Royce's chest. She had once looked at him in such a way, with easy joviality before his hasty, hurtful words had sent her from London and travel abroad. And all because of his brother, and this arse standing next to him who couldn't control their gambling.

Yet they could not entirely be blamed for the family woes. Royce, as head of the family, had not been as careful as one should.

Yet not all was lost. Suzanna had kissed him, after all; perhaps there was hope for them still. He turned his attention back to Henry March. "Would such a decision not be up to Miss March? She is of age, is she not?"

The deadly gleam that entered March's eyes gave Royce an odd sense of pleasure. Annoying the bastard calmed the raging beast inside him that wanted to beat the cocky gentleman to a pulp.

"Seek her out for her fortune, and there will be hell to pay, Danning. Your treatment of her last year was uncalled for and nearly ruined her in the eyes of society. I would see her married to a man she loves and to one who will love her in return. Do I make myself clear?"

Royce chuckled. "And if I love her, will my suit then be welcome?"

"An easy gesture, to profess love to a rich lady when you are broke. You made it obvious she was not acceptable last season. Need I remind you my father established business in textile trading and finance? He worked his way to the wealth and position we hold in society. Or has her fortune blinded you to our common heritage?"

Royce looked away from Suzanna and inhaled a calming breath. "I have not forgotten. But I believe you have also overlooked the fact your sister had a tendre for me, one I wish restored. Keep an eye on her, March; my rakish wiles may see her wedded and bedded before the month is out." He smirked.

"Watch your mouth lest you find yourself wed and dead," March said, with a pointed stare before storming away.

Royce watched March go, and sighed. How he

regretted his words to Suzanna all those months ago. Hated to see her esteem for him wither and die with every hurtful word he'd uttered. His temper, having been spiked by his wayward brother, had been unfairly released on an innocent woman—one who would take much persuasion to believe he meant no harm by his words. It was probably for the best if he left her alone. Just then Suzanna laughed —a warm, wondrous sound—that sent fire coursing toward his groin. Impossible notion, and one he knew he wouldn't adhere to.

Royce looked away and caught sight of his friend, Lord Renn. The Earl waved and strode over.

"Danning, my good man, how have you been? It seems an age since I saw you last."

He scoffed. "If I recall the last time I saw you, Renn, you were disappearing from a ballroom with the married hostess. Who by the way," he said, nodding toward a group of ladies, "is looking in your direction."

Renn laughed. "It was a good night if I remember."

Royce raised an eyebrow at Renn's ignorance to his sarcasm. He shook his head. "What brings you to town? I thought you were for the continent this season?"

"I was. Made it all the way to Spain, then turned for home. Problem with my prized mare. Seems she's fallen pregnant and will not be racing this year after all."

Royce knew very well about prized mares. His gaze sought out Miss March. "Perhaps her foal will be your next great galloper."

Renn snorted. "Highly doubtful when its sire has a tendency for laziness during a race." He took a sip of his drink. "Saw you dancing with Miss March and having a cosy *tête-à-tête* with her brother. Care to enlighten an old friend?"

Royce stifled a growl over the reminder. "March was merely warning me off his sister."

Renn sputtered and choked on his drink. "Like you could possibly be interested in such a disaster. Do you remember last year when she spilt her champagne down the front of her white dress at the Dupree's garden party? But for all her awkwardness, she did have a lovely *décolletage*."

Royce clamped his hands into fists. The last thing he needed to do was lose his temper and come to blows with his best friend before the *ton*. He took a deep calming breath. "I would suggest you forget about Miss March and her awkward first season. I would also recommend your low opinion on Miss March be kept to yourself."

Renn looked at him with astonishment. "You're courting the disaster?"

Anger surged through Royce, and he turned a menacing glare on his soon-to-be ex-friend. "One more word against Miss March, and we are no longer acquaintances," he said, barely controlling his temper. "I wronged her last year and wish to make amends. I've always admired her person. It is just unfortunate she cannot choose her relatives."

"Yes, what a ghastly family. They stink of trade. Why, before her father died I swear he would arrive at entertainments covered in ink." Royce laughed. "I'm surprised Miss March can attend any balls and hold her head up high."

Royce watched Suzanna make her way back to her sibling, her easy graceful movement sure and confident. Last season she would have tripped over her own feet by now and would probably have been trying to stand without showing her ankles. Royce reluctantly admired her transformation into a graceful butterfly. She was a remarkable woman to grace the high sticklers of the *ton* and face them square on. Last season she could barely muster a word without stuttering but not anymore. "I suggest you leave, Renn. Now."

Renn frowned. "Apologies, Danning. I did not know your intentions toward the girl had changed." He cleared his throat. "Do not take offense, old man; who is to look out for you if not I. I am your oldest and best friend. One who, I believe, has the right to remind you the Dannings do not marry those without a title."

"Her brother's a gentleman," Royce said, not bothering to mask his menacing tone. "She is then worthy of my hand by your values."

Renn held his hands up in defeat. "All I meant was the people from trade are different from us. I do not want you to regret a decision you cannot easily mend. I mean, get hold of yourself, Danning; her grandfather was a farmer and not even a gentleman farmer!"

Royce gave his friend a hard look and refused to answer the man's spiteful and lofty principles. He let the taut silence stretch between them.

"Will we see you at Ascot this year?" Renn asked at length.

"No." Royce glared at March across the crowded ballroom, one of the men responsible for his missing the meet. The weight of the debt he owed settled on his shoulders and threatened to crumble him to his knees. "Not this year I'm afraid." Royce pushed the disappointment aside. Such circumstances were wont to happen when one was broke. He should probably start getting used to it.

"Probably a wise move. I hear Jannette is odds-on favourite of winning the Gold Cup. Next year perhaps." Renn signalled to an acquaintance across the room. "I'm off then. Good luck with Miss March or with whatever takes your fancy."

Royce glared at Renn's retreating as he walked away. He didn't appreciate being reminded of her lineage. Lineage that, should his parents still be alive, would never have suited. Yet Suzanna intrigued him. Had done so since the first night he saw her across the room last season, trying to hide behind her aunt and an abundance of fernery. She was sweet but with a strength of character that suited him. All he had to do now was convince her of this fact and see where it took them. Maybe all the way down a church aisle.

"Lost in thought?" her brother asked Suzanna as he came to stand at her side, Victoria clasping his arm.

Suzanna pulled her mind away from the past. "Yes, you could say that."

"Why was Lord Danning sniffing about your skirts?"

"Henry," she admonished. "You should know better than anyone. Lord Danning would not go sniffing about *my* skirts."

"He might with the newly improved Suzanna who now graces the *ton* and lights up every room."

Suzanna slapped her brother's arm with her fan. "Don't be such a tease. His lordship cares for me as much as I care for him, which is naught. He was merely being polite, I imagine."

Her gaze sought Lord Danning, who was bending to talk to a dark-haired beauty in a deep blue gown. "See," she gestured toward his lordship, "he's already found what he sought. I was merely a host's duty and unable to be ignored."

"You would be hard to ignore, Suzanna."

"Thank you, Victoria, you're a dear friend." She swallowed the lump in her throat at the sight of Lord Danning taking the woman out to dance. It was silly, really. Kisses like the one he bestowed were granted, no doubt, many times to other women. To think she had seen or felt anything further in his actions other than lust and need was a notion she should throw to the wind.

"Are you sure he was so very mean last season? Perhaps you caught him at an unfortunate moment."

"Suzanna will not be marrying Viscount Danning, no matter his past or future intentions toward her."

"Why do you hate him so much, Henry?" Suzanna boldly asked. Never had she heard such hatred in her brother's tone.

"I think what he said to you last year is reason enough." He waved the comment away. "In any case, be assured I will not approve of such a choice and would recommend you look elsewhere for a husband."

"First of all, I was never looking at Danning as a suitable candidate in the first place. He spoke to me, and I ended the conversation as quickly as it started. Do not worry yourself over a possibility that will never occur."

"I lost sight of you for a time." Her brother gave her a pointed stare. "Tell me you did not step out with him. You know he's a rake and would probably welcome ruining you now that he realizes the atrocious way he spoke to you last season didn't kill you stone dead in the *ton*."

"Don't be absurd. Lord Danning, for all his politeness —or lack thereof—has not done me any damage this eve." *Besides kissing her senseless.*

Victoria looked at her with narrowed eyes before she turned toward the dancing couples. "I see he's dancing with Lady Flintstock, an heiress from Cumberland, I believe," she said with a consoling smile.

"Yes, a thorough and pure lady with a title that stretches back to Queen Elizabeth." Suzanna sighed.

"She has a rather pinched face, though, don't you agree?" her brother asked, one eyebrow raised.

Suzanna frowned. "Henry you should know better than to be so insensitive. At least she's not tarnished."

"You are not tarnished, Suzanna. Unless there is something you are not telling me." Henry met her gaze.

"No," she said, clasping her brother's arm, and hoping a blush, over what she'd done earlier, didn't bloom on her cheeks. "I only meant we are tarnished...by trade."

"Oh, of course, how could I forget." Her brother laughed. "But better that, my dear, than tarnished by debt."

CHAPTER 5

"Lady Victoria to see you, Miss Suzanna."

Suzanna looked up from her latest *La Belle Assemblée*, and noted the time. "Tea, please, Peter and have cook plate up some macaroons. I know they're one of Lady Victoria's favourites."

"Yes, miss." The butler dipped his head and departed. A smile quirked her lips at the sound of Victoria's slippered feet patting across the parquetry foyer floor. She was a loyal and wonderful friend, and after the questioning look Victoria had bestowed on her at the ball last week, Suzanna had been waiting for her to call.

"Beautiful weather we're having, Suzanna," Victoria said, coming toward her and kissing her cheeks. "Perhaps tomorrow we could persuade Henry to take us out in the carriage, perhaps a turnabout Hyde Park? What do you say?"

"Sounds like a marvellous idea. I'm sure Henry would agree."

They sat on the settee before the unlit hearth. Victoria pulled her gloves off and placed them on the table, then turned to her. A knowing silence stretched between them.

With a resounding sigh, Victoria spoke. "At the ball last week, I saw you step out with Lord Danning and not reappear until sometime later. What were you up to?"

"Nothing of consequence." Suzanna paused, her mind a whir of excuses. "He apologized for his treatment and harsh words last season. That was all."

"Why are you blushing then? I am your dearest and best friend, so please tell me. I would never dishonour you by telling anyone else, if that is your concern."

Suzanna slumped back into the settee. The overwhelming urge to confide in her friend was too much to resist. "He kissed me. Well, actually, we seemed to kiss each other at the same time. One moment, we were arguing and then the next I had an urge to show him what he threw away." Suzanna touched her lips remembering the feel of him, his ardent mouth, and his roaming hands that sent shivers down her spine even now. Her cheeks burned.

"You kissed Lord Danning! Oh my." Victoria made a play of fanning herself. "What was it like?"

Suzanna smiled. "Marvellous. His lips were quite energetic and able. But then.... He did the oddest thing and used his tongue. It was most interesting and made my stomach feel as if butterflies were taking flight within."

"That does sound marvellous but a little strange. Will you be doing it again, do you think?" Victoria's eyes were wide with excitement.

"No." Suzanna frowned, as her answer brought forth a deep emptiness inside. "Well, perhaps if he bestows such liberties again on me. You know I could never initiate such wantonness myself."

"Why do you think he kissed you? After his words last season...."

It was a question Suzanna had been asking herself. Perhaps Lord Danning was sorry for his rudeness and really wished to make amends. And being a rake of the highest calibre, perhaps kissing innocent women was his way of making it up to them.

"I'm not entirely sure," she answered in all honesty. "Perchance he is truly sorry. He certainly seemed sincere."

Victoria chuckled and rose from her seat, pacing before the hearth. "I think you should play a little game with Lord Danning. He was rude and uncouth last year to be sure and now he should pay a penalty for his behaviour. I think," Victoria pulled Suzanna to her feet, "that you should dangle yourself before him, make him realize what he has thrown away, and can no longer have. Tease him shamelessly."

Suzanna stilled, hearing a plan she herself had thought to accomplish the eve of the kiss; before Lord Danning and his wicked lips had taken her senses and decorum and thrown them into the cesspit of loose morals and gentlemanly needs.

"Are you telling me, Victoria, you think I should kiss him again? That such behaviour would be something with which you concur when a woman's been slighted as I?"

Her friend grinned and nodded. "That is exactly what I think you should do. It's about time we women stood up for ourselves and were no longer seen as a commodity to be bought when a gentleman has tired of his latest *chère-amie*."

"This is such a wicked plan." Suzanna paused. "His kisses were very nice, but what shall I do if he tries to take my favours further?"

"You are a sensible woman. I know you'll not allow it to proceed too far. And then when the season ends and you receive a proposal from Lord Danning, you may give him his *congé* and marry someone else. And serves him right, too," Victoria said with a decisive nod.

The thought of the proud Lord Danning heartbroken and at Suzanna's feet, tears running down his strong, unshaven jaw.... No, such an image didn't suit him at all. She shook the reflection away. He'd more than likely shrug and head to Whites for a game of cards and a glass of their finest brandy.

"Very well, I'll dangle myself before him like a ripe mouse before a cat and we'll see if he walks into my trap. What do I have to lose?"

"Well, your reputation, my dear, should anyone find out about the game you're playing with Lord Danning. You must be discreet, that is foremost important. Yet you should also make him believe he could receive further favours from you other than kissing, yet never in reality. Oh, this will be such fun. You must promise to keep me informed," Victoria begged, clasping her hands, only restraining her excitement when a footman brought in the tea tray. Her friend's eyes lit up when she spied the macaroons. "Oh, you're a dearest, Suzanna. You know how much I love macaroons."

Suzanna laughed, poured the tea, and ensured Victoria had an ample serving of her favourite sweet. "So where do you think I should start my plan of seduction?"

"Oh yes, *seduction* is just the right word to use," Victoria said, her gaze bright with mischief and the crumbs of her macaroon speckling her lips. "The Staffon's ball is three days away. Lord Danning is sure to be there, as will you."

"Yes, Aunt Agnes has already started to worry about the engagement. You know how she is in such company." Suzanna bit into a macaroon and wondered how her aunt would handle one of the biggest events of this season.

"Mama will be attending with me; and she will keep your aunt company. Do not worry, Suzanna."

"Thank you, Victoria, you're a true friend."

"That I am, my dearest. One who is determined to see you marry well while at the same time bring the high and mighty Lord Danning to his knees. He shall pine forever over the loss of you."

It was what Suzanna wanted as well as long as she did not encourage an entanglement ending in her ruination.

⚜

Three days later, Suzanna stood alone watching Lord Danning from across the room at the Staffon's ball. Unaware of her gaze, he moved through the *ton* like a predator stalking its next meal. Little did he know he was going to be hers.

Tonight, he wore a shadow across his jaw that made him seem more wild and roguish than normal. Given his reputation in the *ton* already, many a woman's head turned at the sight of him and Suzanna was no different. She couldn't look away from him. He might not be easy to seduce, but he would be worth the effort—she was sure.

One taste of him had proven that.

Dressed in white silk, Suzanna blended with the many white-clad women privileged with an invitation. Lady Staffon always stipulated her guests wear one colour of her choice to her balls, whereas the hostess was free to wear any colour she chose. Blue was her choice this evening with a gown that drew the eye of many a gentleman, and Lord Danning was no exception.

Suzanna frowned as his lordship's gaze lowered on the bountiful *décolletage* of the married hostess for longer than was deemed proper as if any time at all was deemed proper to view another lady's breasts. She gazed down at her own cleavage and wondered if there was enough there with which to tease him. Certainly, the other night he had seemed pleased with her person. The rake obviously had some sort of tendre for that part of a woman's anatomy.

How strange....

"You look beautiful, Suzanna. Do not worry; as soon as Lord Danning sees you, my dear, he will make his way over. Why, you've already danced with many a gentleman, enough to cause even our hostess to become a little jealous."

"He has not noticed me yet." Suzanna met Victoria's gaze and raised her brows. "Perhaps a plan of seduction was wishful thinking on my part."

"Nonsense. He has only just arrived. Give him time." Her friend paused and took a sip of her champagne. "Is your brother coming tonight?"

"No. He said he had a previous engagement." Suzanna looked out into the throng and met the heavy-lidded stare of Lord Danning leaning against the wall. She took in his fine skin-tight breeches that left nothing of what lay beneath to the imagination. Not to mention his wide shoulders and large hands...hands that had been against her body, pulling her close, and touching her with a reverence that still left her breathless.

"See, my dear. Here he comes."

So lost in her perusal of him, Suzanna hadn't noticed him walking their way. Oh dear, what would she say to the man? Now the time had come to play the siren, she wasn't at all sure she was capable of such antics. It was one thing to think she could do such things but quite another to actually do them.

She looked away from the delectable sight he made and watched the elderly Lord Bromley dance with his wife, thirty years his junior. A disturbing sight, sure to pull one's mind away from what was bearing down on her with belly-tensing speed.

"Good evening, Lady Victoria, Miss March," Lord Danning said with a slight bow. Suzanna curtsied and took in his smouldering eyes. Embarrassment swamped her when she realized his gaze was not directed at her but her friend.

"Good evening, Lord Danning." Victoria glanced her way, before looking back to his lordship. "Are you enjoying the ball, my lord?"

"I am, my lady and ever more so now that I may have the delightful pleasure of dancing with you."

A flush rose on her friends cheeks. "Oh, I hadn't thought to dance tonight, my lord."

At Victoria's attempt to dissuade Lord Danning, Suzanna took pity on her friend and the awkward silence that settled about them all. "You should enjoy the evening. I'll find your mama and sit with her."

"Are you sure? I don't wish to leave you alone." Victoria frowned.

Suzanna quickly met Lord Danning's eyes and smiled. The gesture was all she could summon due to the lump wedged in her throat. "Of course," she said quickly. "In fact I've just spotted your mama. I will see you a little later." And with a quick curtsy, Suzanna moved toward the ballroom doors with no intention of seeking out Victoria's mama.

Cool air hit her face as she moved into the less crowded passageway, a welcome reprieve from the overcrowded stifling ballroom. She leaned against the wall and caught her breath that seemed to be coming in rapid repetition.

What a silly fool she was, to imagine Lord Danning would fall for her. A ridiculous notion she should never have contemplated. To think she had been going to seduce him and play him for a fool. Yet, once again he had trumped her ace. No, squashed her under his leather top-boots like an annoying little ant not worth his notice. She had presented herself like a wanton hussy and heat stole up her neck at the thought. Not that she did anything terribly wrong. Yet one should never allow rakes to kiss them in the way he had last week in the garden.

Suzanna pushed away from the wall and ambled toward the retiring room. No one spoke to her when she made her way to a window seat overlooking the darkened garden and stared out at her reflection on the glass.

Perhaps being here, among the highest London peerage, was a foolish notion. Yet tonight she seemed popular with the gentlemen; but more than likely her acceptance this eve was solely due to arriving with Victoria's mama, the Countess of Ross.

The lump was back in her throat and tears welled. She wiped them away and sniffed. What lunacy to think she could find a husband in this society. Yes, she had wealth but what of it when no one cared about nor welcomed such a family into their lives.

She needed a change of scenery.

No longer would she refuse the abundant cards of the lower society that arrived daily and sat unopened on her brother's desk. At least by marrying a gentleman from her own sphere, her chances of marrying for love and not for some Lord's financial gain were in her favour.

Calm settled about her like a comforting hug. It was the right decision, a decision long overdue.

The *ton* could go hang.

R oyce stood at the side of the Tattersall's auction ring and fought not to lose his decorum. All morning the auctioneer slammed down the hammer like a death knell on his prized horseflesh and vehicles. With every item sold, Royce cursed himself and his brother to Hades.

His friend, Lord Renn, was even here, purchasing his prized horseflesh without a flicker of remorse. Self-disgust ate at him, the feeling lying heavily on his shoulders.

It was a sobering day.

"With the horse sales, the harvest reaping, and the sale of your Rome estate, I do believe you'll see your financial situation to rights, my lord."

Royce glanced at his solicitor tallying away in his notebook. He cringed as the final hammer gong came down on his champion two-year old, Kingstar. There went his racing season. His temper soared when the even-tempered colt was led from the arena by Suzanna's brother, Mr. Henry March.

"Bastard."

"Pardon, my lord?" His solicitor gazed at him in concern.

"Nothing." Royce marched over to the auctioneer and thanked him for his services before returning to his man of business. "Pay off the most pressing debts immediately, and send word to me of who is left to pay. Write to them and see if they will hold off until the harvest is in. It is not too much to ask, surely." Royce could only hope the debtors agreed.

"Yes, my lord." His solicitor nodded and sauntered toward his carriage. Royce walked out onto the street and realized he no longer had the luxury of such a vehicle. Hailing a hackney cab, he jumped in and threw himself onto the squabs. The smell of tobacco and vomit wafted from the seat.

Royce shook his head and lowered the cab's window, disgusted by the odour that would ruin his suit. This would never do. How could he continue to grace society when all would be privy to him selling off his horses and carriages? To explain away such an action would be impossible. The *ton* would never believe the excuse he merely wished to renew his stock. They would see through his lie like a piece of glass.

Royce yelled out his direction to the driver and clasped the belt above the window as the carriage rumbled over the cobbled road. His thoughts turned to his brother whom he'd not seen these past four days.

He frowned.

CHAPTER 6

O ver the following weeks, Suzanna attended many balls and parties of London's gentry' society. Henry, happy to see her away from the money-hungry rakes of the upper London *ton*, attended with her and made the necessary introductions when required.

It was very liberating, Suzanna found, to be the most sought after and highly regarded, among their set. The only drawback was Victoria's absence from her side. Being an earl's daughter, her friend circulated in a different sphere to the one Suzanna now called home.

"Penny for your thoughts, Suzanna."

With a sigh, she looked across at her brother seated in the family carriage. His eyes and his white cravat were the only parts she could make out of him in the darkened space. "Just a penny? You're turning cheap, Henry." At his resounding chuckle, Suzanna laughed. "I was just thinking of how much I miss Victoria and yet not her society at all."

"We are as good as anyone else." Henry shifted on his seat, a sign of his aggravation at the reminder of their heritage. "Our money may have come from the hard work of our father, but his fortune was honestly earned and not to be considered lightly. I wager, had a high and mighty lord needed your fortune desperately enough, his dearest mama would have been easy enough to buy. Makes me sick, thinking of you marrying a rogue who is only after your purse. To risk having you thrust into a family who, after access to your blunt, may have treated you abominably."

Suzanna sighed, one rogue in particular coming to mind although Lord Danning had no need for her money. What a shame he didn't attend some of the balls of her new sphere. He would then see what a catch she was, even if not to his taste.

"I understand Mr. Jenkins will be in attendance this evening."

"Really," Suzanna said, trying to hide the boredom that entered her voice at the mention of the man. A baron's third son who thought she would make him a perfect wife, whether affection was involved or not. Not in her case.

Had she not escaped to her brother's side two evenings past, Suzanna was sure she'd still be trapped in Mrs. Hill's supper room, listening to him preach about the appalling gravel paths in Hyde Park and how he'd tripped over a pebble some days past. Pity the boring man wouldn't fall into the Serpentine and disappear altogether. "How fortunate for us," she said.

Henry grinned. "So you won't be marrying the poor fellow, then?"

"Certainly not." Suzanna met her brother's laughing gaze. "And I expect if he comes to call, you will let him down gently and save him the embarrassment of hearing it from me."

"I will do no such thing, Suzanna. If he asks, you will

do your duty and tell him *no* yourself. In any case," he said, checking his cravat and picking up his hat, "you should be warned, it is not only Mr. Jenkins who's been looking at you for a wife. Many gentlemen have approached me and asked of you. Surely one of them meets your favour?"

"Not yet," she said, clasping the seat as the carriage rocked to a halt. "But I'll let you know when one does."

"Marvellous." Henry's reply cloaked in sarcasm. "Now come; dinner awaits."

Suzanna entered the foyer of Baronet Blyth's Belgravia home. With the help of a footman, she shrugged off her cloak and took her brother's arm. Sir William and his wife, Lady Blyth, greeted them warmly at the drawing room door before ushering them inside. Footmen bustled about, serving hors d'oeuvres and drinks to the gathered throng. Suzanna glanced about the room to see who was present. Her steps faltered.

"He's a cad," her brother growled through his teeth. "If he thinks I'll give you away to him, he has rocks in his head."

Suzanna patted his arm and smiled as they came up to a group of ladies of her acquaintance. "I'm sure he has a reason for being present. I highly doubt it's because of me."

"Suzanna," he said, pulling her to a stop. "You would make a most suitable and equal wife to Viscount Danning. And he knows it. I've no doubt he is here because of you. Tell me," he paused, looking over her shoulder, his eyes narrowing in the direction of his lordship, "have you ever seen him in this society before?"

She frowned and shook her head. "No."

"Neither have I. But the moment you step away from the *ton*, he comes crawling into our sphere like a dog sniffing out a wealthy bone."

"Don't be so rude, Henry. Lord Danning, for whatever

reason, is here as a guest of Sir Blyth. You must be polite or I'll tell Victoria what a grouch of a husband you will make." Suzanna chuckled at the blush that rose on her brother's cheeks.

"You're a cruel woman, Suzanna."

She smiled and pulled him toward her new friends. "Not cruel at all and you know it. Just making sure you behave like the gentleman I know you to be."

Sometime later, Henry escorted her into dinner where, much to Suzanna's despair, she was deposited beside Lord Danning. Henry, seated across from her, threw his lordship a baleful glare before turning to the entree before him.

"So this is where you have been hiding over the last few weeks, Miss March." Lord Danning looked about the room with a studied air.

"I thought a change of society would do me well, my lord, and up until this eve it had done so." He smiled and Suzanna immediately regretted her politely worded set down. Having told her brother to act the gentleman, she had been unable to hold her own tongue.

"Lady Victoria misses you greatly, I believe. Will you ever come back and light up our ballrooms as you once did?"

A spike of irrational jealousy shot through her at the thought of Victoria airing her feelings to Lord Danning and receiving condolences in return. It was silly of her; Lord Danning could speak with whomever he wished; she was nothing to him. And Victoria was her friend and she should not think ill of her over a man. Especially this man. "I saw Victoria only last week, my lord. I do believe you are exaggerating."

"On the contrary, Miss March. Why, only last eve while dancing a waltz with her she told me how she wished you were there. Of course, I concurred and said I would take it upon myself to find out where you had gone and what you find so favourable to keep you away."

Barely repressing her temper, Suzanna placed down her spoon and turned toward the vexing man at her side. "Well, now you have found me. Do not let me be the one to hold you from your entertainments. You see, I happen to like this society and the people who grace it. As for the last sphere I graced, other than Victoria, I cannot say there was anything else to recommend it."

Lord Danning clasped his chest. "You wound my fragile heart."

Her eyes narrowed and she took a calming breath. "What are you really doing here, Lord Danning?"

He smiled and sipped his wine. "I've come to see you. I've missed you."

"Really?" Suzanna chuckled, the sound tinged with sarcasm. "You're a liar and a rogue, my lord. And if you think I will fall for your pretty words, you're sadly mistaken."

He grinned. "Has anyone ever told you how beautiful you are when you're angry? Your temper suits the fiery colour of your hair."

Suzanna looked about the table in fear of others hearing his lordship's inappropriate compliment. She shushed him. "Perhaps you should heed the warning my hair is giving you then, my lord. And in any case, you're wasting your flattery on me." The feel of satin knee breeches, a knee in particular, rubbed suggestively against her leg. Suzanna struggled to swallow her mouthful of soup as her breath caught in her lungs. Her body longed to feel the man beside her and she quickly squashed the emotion like a bug.

"In all honesty, I came because Sir Blyth is one of my

oldest and dearest friends. We attended Cambridge together."

Suzanna swallowed and met Lord Danning's eye before looking about the table. She had not known he had such a friendship with Sir Blyth. It would explain the genial banter between the two before dinner. To know he did not decry the middle aristocratic class placed him in a slightly more favourable light.

Only slightly.

"You're surprised?" he asked, mirth visible in his dark-blue orbs.

Suzanna shrugged. "Of course I am, my lord. I wouldn't have thought," she said in a lowered voice, "Sir Blyth was deemed good *ton*."

"He isn't, by high society's standards but by mine, of course."

He smiled as the first course was cleared from before them. His appreciative study of her made her stomach somersault, reminding her of the night they were together on the terrace....

"You shouldn't look at me like so, my lord. It's disconcerting."

He chuckled but said nothing. Nor did he need for Suzanna to know what he was thinking. The very same thoughts as she was having. Of them locked together under an ivy vine, his hands against her flesh, holding her captive to an onslaught of desire, which until that night was unknown to her.

Suzanna reached for her water and fumbling, spilled the entire drink on the white, highly starched tablecloth. Heat bloomed on her face and as she stood to avoid the liquid spilling onto her skirt, she heard a resounding thud —her chair crashing against the floorboards.

"I'm so sorry, Sir Blyth. I'm so clumsy." Unable to still

the tremor running though her hands, Suzanna tried to mop up the abundant spill with her napkin.

Sir Blyth waved her concerns away and summoned a footman. "Please see to the mess, and fetch Miss March another glass of water."

Suzanna slumped onto her chair and when she sat into nothing but thin air, wished the ground would open up and swallow her whole. All the humiliations of last season came crashing down, along with the remains of her dinner, when her hands shot out to clasp anything to stop her fall.

Shouts and gasps sounded about her. Suzanna looked down at her ruined gown, covered in the *entrée*. The multi-coloured stain also covered most of her bosom.

Unable to stop herself, she looked up at Lord Danning, whose visage was impossible to read. She pushed away his offer of help and gained her feet, striding from the room with all the dignity she could muster, willing her feet to take her far from the scene of such complete humiliation. All those months and money spent on making her a lady who fit the *ton* and all its lofty ideals were for nothing. She had not changed; she was still the unlucky debutante from last season.

At the sound of voices and footsteps from behind, Suzanna rushed down the hallway and fled into the ladies retiring room. She shut the door and leaned against it in the hopes whoever had followed her would be discouraged and leave her alone. When the door opened with an almighty shove, she was thrown face down onto the Aubusson rug. It seemed such a wish was not to be granted this eve.

· · ·

"Suzanna, I do apologize. Here," Royce said, leaning down and pulling her to stand. "I would never have barged in had I known you were standing behind the door." He watched her right her clothes as best she could before she turned, sauntered over to a basin of water, and tried to wipe the remains of her dinner from her gown.

Suzanna glared at him over her shoulder as a blob of sauce dropped and splattered onto the floor. "My clothes are already soiled, so landing on the floor for a second time this evening will not matter."

His gaze stole over her ruined apparel and the sad, unsure woman he had known last year stared back at him across the room. An ache settled in his chest at the dishevelled picture she made. All of which was his fault. Had he not tried to fluster her by touching her leg, she would not have suffered such humiliation.

"I apologize if my actions earlier this night upset you to the point you spilled—"

"My drink. All over the table before falling on my backside in front of the dinner guests I was trying to impress. Since," she walked over to him and poked his chest with a finger, "the society I had initially graced wanted naught to do with me and all because of a certain pompous, arrogant, high-in-the-instep lord."

Royce sighed. Her tone did not bode well for his plan to win Suzanna and make her his wife. "Like I said, I apologize. Perhaps for me to make amends, you would agree to a ride in the park tomorrow. I believe the weather is to be congenial."

"Unlike the company," she stated, with a narrow, piercing stare that could have turned him to ash on the Aubusson rug beneath his boots.

"There's no need to be...." Her eyes narrowed further

as Royce cut off what he was about to say. He doubted his suggestion that she should be polite would place her in a more pleasant mood.

"You should leave, my lord. If you could find my brother and send him in, I would be appreciative."

Royce tucked a flyaway curl behind her ear and noted for the first time a delightful mole above her slightly parted and lusciously plump lip. She was mouth-watering in this dishevelled state. A little of the soup clung to a strand of her hair, and he had an overwhelming urge to clean it away. She pulled away from his hand.

"And you may stop looking at me like that, Lord Danning." She ambled toward the window and fumbled with the heavy velvet drapes drawn closed for the evening. "I know I may make interesting sport for a rake of the *ton*, but I refuse to allow you to laugh at my clumsiness or make me cry any longer. I want you to leave."

Royce watched her attempt to hold her composure and a fear unlike any he had ever known assailed him. He'd made her cry?

"Suzanna, don't be upset." He took a step toward her.

"How can I not be upset? You purposefully toyed with me at dinner, to the point where I again became that clumsy freckled redheaded girl who hails from trade with not an ounce of breeding or the decorum to suit your exalted sphere. You made the society in which I belong scorn me."

"They would not think such a thing, especially Sir and Lady Blyth. Two people I hold in high regard."

"Of course, you would say such a thing. You're a Viscount, lord of all you survey. They would not dare naysay or slight you."

"You're wrong," Royce said, unable to believe the venomous tone of Suzanna's words.

"Am I? I'm not so sure." She turned from the window, and Royce noted her glassy, bright eyes. She started for the exit and he knew he couldn't let her go, believing what she said. Royce stepped in front of the door and refused to permit her to leave.

"Get out of my way."

"I cannot. I've made you cry. Please, Suzanna, don't be angry or distressed at my foolish attempt to seduce you. I never meant you harm."

She glared at him for what seemed an age, the dislike in her green depths as murky as the sea. Then the crack of her hand slapping his skin echoed loudly in the room. Royce stood still, shocked to his core. Never had he been slapped by a person in his entire life. Not even his stern father had laid a hand against him during his childhood. And God knows he'd deserved it at times. The experience was quite...novel, even if it did sting like the blazes.

"Why did you do that?"

"Move, or I'll do it again. You deserved it, you cad."

She tried to move about him, and he clasped her arms to hold her still. Her skin, the colour of alabaster, was soft under his hands. Her upper arms were so slight he was able to wrap his hands fully about them. "I am not a cad. I may have certain rakish wiles but I'm not a cad." At her shocked gasp over his words, he frowned. "Why don't you like me?"

"I've already told you why, Lord Danning. There is nothing more to be said on the subject."

Royce thought there was plenty yet to say but her upturned nose indicated she was ignoring him. "Miss Suzanna March, if you are so determined to leave me to this ladies retiring room, would you allow me one wish?"

"I certainly will not." Suzanna met his gaze and then quickly looked away.

"Suzanna, may I kiss you goodnight?"

Her eyes widened and Royce seized the opportunity her shocked countenance afforded him. He took her lips and again, he was shocked at how sweet and innocent they tasted, a heady mixture that sent his senses reeling and his body longing for more. She opened for him, sighing into his mouth at their joining.

He walked her until the retiring room door stood at her back. Using the doors support, he lifted her leg a little to sit against his hip. Her body beneath the fine silk gown was perfection, and he reveled in the feel of her soft skin. How he'd love to pull the stockings from her long legs with his teeth, to taste and conquer the delicacies that awaited him between her legs.

She gasped at their closeness, his breathing as ragged as hers. His cock stood to attention and he rubbed it against her sex, pulling back a little to watch as her emerald eyes opened in awe.

Moving, he teased them both, her hands spiking through his hair to bring his lips back to hers, kissing *him* this time, and leaving him in unknown waters he'd never sailed before, where emotions ran riot, and need overtook want.

His hand strayed to her ass and he felt the moment her propriety pulled her back from the brink of pleasure. She pushed him away, striding toward a small writing desk on the opposite side of the room.

"Why do you always use seduction as a means to coerce? I'm not a toy to be messed about and thrown away when I'm no longer fun. I am so angry at you I could throw this paperweight at your head. And I certainly should never have kissed you."

Royce rubbed his jaw. "My apologies, Suzanna. Truly. It is just whenever I'm in your presence I cannot help myself. I like you. I like you very much." He sighed and walked toward her. Suzanna's gaze was wary, yet she did not move away. "I've always thought you a beautiful woman. You are kind and gentle, not a common affection found in the *ton*." He clasped her gloved hand and was thankful she did not pull it away. "You are a lady of the first water who I would like to know better."

Her eyes bored into his as if to try and seek the lie she was sure he told. She would find none; what he spoke was the truth.

"You were so rude to me last season. You cut me stone dead in the ballroom before so many people. Why did you do it? I thought we were friends."

Royce pulled her toward a settee and sat. "It wasn't you I was mad at. You found me at an unfortunate moment. My behaviour was not gentlemanly, and I apologize for the pain I caused you. I never meant to hurt you, or make you believe I thought you beneath me because of your family connections."

"What was so wrong that you reacted in such a way with me?"

Royce frowned. The last thing he wanted Suzanna to know was her brother had been the cause of his ill humour and part of the reason for his family's financial strife. The inability of both of their brothers to cease gambling and wasting time in the dens of London had caused him to snap at her. Hurt her.

He met her gaze and swallowed the lump of a lie which threatened to choke him. To tell her the truth now could ruin the delicate truce they'd seemed to form in the last few minutes. He couldn't risk losing her now, not through the fault of others. She did not need to be privy to his problems.

"It was a private matter I've since dealt with...or am dealing with, I should say. You mustn't concern yourself."

She smiled but something in her eyes told Royce she didn't wholly believe him. "So," he said, wanting to change the subject. "Will you ride with me tomorrow?"

"Where?"

"If you're in agreement, I'd like you to take the air with me around Hyde Park," he asked.

Suzanna eyed him for a moment then shrugged. "Why are you doing this, Lord Danning? Are we to be friends again, then?"

He nodded. "It is certainly something I wish." He paused. "And perhaps being seen with me may help you gain favour back in the *ton* should I have damaged it in any way in the past." The *ton* could go hang itself as far as Royce cared but it seemed to be something important to Suzanna, and if it persuaded her to join him on an outing he was clever enough to use the ruse.

She stared at him and her dishevelled state made her look uncommonly pretty. Unable to deny himself, Royce lent in and kissed her in a quick embrace he wished could go on forever. He pulled back and stared at Suzanna as his body roared with need, bucked at its denial of her, yet something more also simmered under his skin. A need to protect. To care.

"I suppose I could." Suzanna stood and walked to the door. Royce took the opportunity to watch her hips sway in an unconscious seduction. He tore his gaze from her derriere.

"I'll be ready at five o'clock. Don't be late," Suzanna added.

He stood, and bowed. "Until tomorrow, Miss March."

"Good night, my lord."

CHAPTER 7

"You are not stepping outside this house in the company of that rogue."

Suzanna gritted her teeth against her brother's dictate, one she intended to ignore. "You may be my brother, but Lord Danning is an eligible gentleman and one with whom I choose to associate."

"Why would you want to step out with a man who only last year caused you so much heartache? Don't try and fool me into believing he wasn't the reason you hightailed it to Paris." Henry slumped into the chair behind his desk and ran a hand over his face. "Explain to me why you would wish to do such a thing."

Suzanna frowned and wondered at her reasoning. Lord Danning had been cruel, but something urged her to give him a second chance. Had she not also, on occasion, snapped at the people she loved when out of sorts and in ill humour? "Lord Danning has apologized and explained our unfortunate interaction last season to my satisfaction. And let us not forget to be seen with a viscount could sway the *haute ton* to see me in a more favourable light, and not a lady covered in ink. I need to find a husband, Henry. I cannot live with you forever, not to mention Aunt Agnes is getting on in age."

"You say you are satisfied and believe this rubbish Viscount Danning spouts?"

"Of course," she said. "Why does that surprise you?"

"Because he's a money-hungry rogue only after your fortune, and he's in queer street up to his haughty eyebrows."

Suzanna ambled over to the window that looked out onto Curzon Street and watched polished carriages pass by, their wheels rumbling over the cobbled road. "You don't know that."

"I do and you will not marry him."

At her brother's stern expression, Suzanna smiled. "Of course I will not. I believe this carriage outing is only a means to apologize. No reason for you to go into a state of panic. I'll be back within the hour." At her statement, a highly polished curricle stopped before the house and excitement skittered across Suzanna's skin. "His lordship is here. I'll see you in an hour or so."

"Suzanna?"

"Yes?" she asked, stopping at the library door.

"You deserve a marriage of love, not one that will serve only to fill some rogue's coffers. He is after your money, my dear, no matter what sonnets or other pretty words he sings."

"I'm determined to marry for love, Henry, and I will. I'll not be drawn in, I promise you." She blew him a kiss and left, hoping her anticipation at seeing Lord Danning again was entirely platonic.

Yet knowing her eagerness was not.

"You look delightful, Miss March," Lord Danning said as he settled beside her on the bench. He picked up the ribbons and flicked them over the haunches of his two matched greys, which stood stomping in place.

"Thank you. Such flattery, my lord."

"It is no more than the truth." He grinned and her legs felt like jelly.

She tried to ignore the compliment and the heat flaming her cheeks by studying their surroundings. Carriages busy with afternoon trade pulled onto the roads around them, weaving through the traffic trying to gain their destination in the quickest possible time.

Lord Danning seemed unfazed and handled his pair with ease. Soon the gates of Hyde Park came into view and so, too, members of the *ton* taking the air this warm spring day.

"I believe Lady Victoria will be in the park. Do you wish to see her?"

"Of course," Suzanna said, a little dejected at the realization Lord Danning was keeping a record of her friend's whereabouts.

"I heard her mention it at a ball I attended after I left the dinner party last eve." He held her gaze. "I do not wish to court her."

Suzanna shrugged. "Why should you not court her? She is a woman of your station and of an age to marry. She would make you a very fine wife."

"I don't desire Lady Victoria as my bride, nor do I hold romantic inclinations towards her."

At the deep huskiness in his voice, Suzanna reminded herself she was there to be seen, not to start a flirtation with the viscount. She cleared her throat. "There are many people about today."

Lord Danning chuckled. "Yes, there are."

They drove for a time in quiet before, unable to stand the silence any longer, Suzanna inquired, "And have you any plans for this evening?"

"Yes, I am attending the Moncroft's masquerade."

"I do believe we were invited." Suzanna stifled a gasp as Lord Danning's thigh brushed hers and a bolt of awareness shot throughout her body. She shifted aside and fidgeted with her gloves, hoping he hadn't noticed her reaction to his closeness. After his kiss the other night, all she could think of was being so close again, of him touching her, devouring her in every delicious way.

"Well, you must attend." Lord Danning manoeuvred the carriage to the side of the path so another could pass before he turned to her, his dark eyes hooded with an emotion she could not name. "I would love to waltz with you, Miss March."

"Suzanna, please, my lord. Miss March can sound so droll at times."

He laughed, and another shiver of delight stole over her body. Why did his voice make her react in such a way? "You do understand I view our newfound friendship as just a friendship, my lord?"

He smiled and looked away. "If it is what you wish, then of course I'll honour your wishes."

Suzanna gazed at his lordship and noted her words had somehow stripped warmth from his gaze. At the sound of laughter, she looked toward a copse of trees and saw Victoria walking some distance before her mama's carriage with a gentleman Suzanna did not recognize.

"That is Mr. Swinson, an American from New York. He's rich as Croesus and only too eager to publicize the fact."

"By the tone of your voice I gather you do not like the gentleman, my lord?"

"No, I do not. He's a gambler."

Suzanna frowned at the hateful tone of Lord Danning's words. "You do not approve of gamblers or the vice?"

"Not at all, but to lose one's fortune and estates which generations before you have worked hard to keep," he said, meeting her gaze, "is the worst kind of treachery."

"I agree," Suzanna said. "Seems such a useless thing to do. I am so fortunate to have a brother who stays well clear of such London dens."

"Really?"

At Lord Danning's sarcastic tone, Suzanna met his gaze and frowned. "Well of course. Henry has assured me on many an occasion he does not partake in that gentlemanly pursuit."

Lord Danning manoeuvred the curricle to a halt not far from where Victoria strolled with Mr. Swinson and ordered his tiger to hold the horses.

Suzanna ignored the warm comforting heat of his lordship's hand as he helped her step from the carriage. Even the leather of her glove was no impediment to the effect he had on her. It was unlike anything she'd ever experienced before. *Damn him.*

Victoria rushed toward them. "Suzanna, I was hoping to meet you here. Lord Danning told me you were to ride with him today."

"Victoria," she said, kissing her friend's cheek. "I too am glad to see you." Suzanna looked at Mr. Swinson and smiled.

"Oh, let me introduce you. This is Mr. Swinson, a friend of my father's from New York. Mr. Swinson, this is my oldest and dearest friend, Miss Suzanna March."

Suzanna curtsied, then immediately found her hand placed neatly on Lord Danning's arm. She met Victoria's laughing gaze and strove not to blush. The gesture, as sweet as it appeared, merely indicated his lordship was a gentleman and nothing more.

"We were about to walk down to the Serpentine. Would you care to join us?" Victoria smiled and Suzanna noted Mr. Swinson's appreciative gaze linger on her friend.

Suzanna looked to Lord Danning. He nodded. "We would be pleased to join you, Lady Victoria," he said.

They strolled the grassy bank that led to the water, the sunlight warm and comforting on their skin.

"I've heard Moncroft's ball will be a crush once again. I do not understand why he sends out so many invitations when his modest ballroom can only hold so many."

Suzanna chuckled at her friend's annoyance. "To have a crush is the thing, don't you know, Victoria," she said.

"True, I suppose, but it doesn't make for a comfortable evening."

"I wholeheartedly agree, Lady Victoria," said Mr. Swinson, his native tongue sounding foreign in the English setting. "I, for one, could think of a better way to pass an evening."

"Such as?" Lord Danning asked, the aggravation in his tone in no way veiled.

Eyebrows raised, Mr. Swinson looked at Lord Danning. Suzanna held her breath as the two men seemed to take the other's measure.

"Well, to spend a night with a select group of friends, for one." Mr. Swinson answered. "Perhaps the partaking of dancing and cards."

"Hmm." Lord Danning paused. "You run a printing company in New York, I understand. What is it that brings you to London?"

Suzanna met Victoria's eyes and noted her friend's unease over the barely disguised dislike between the two men. Had Suzanna not known better, she would think Lord Danning jealous. Did his lordship like Victoria and disagree with her association with the American? Was his denial of attraction to her friend a lie? Or was it because Mr. Swinson was in trade and therefore beneath notice?

"Pleasure, mostly." Mr. Swinson smiled at Victoria. "And to see Lord Ross, of course. As you are well aware, his lordship is an old friend of my father's. Then I shall travel to Paris. I'm looking to start a woman's fashion magazine."

"Sounds exciting," Victoria stated.

"I wish you well with your endeavours, Mr. Swinson." Suzanna smiled in all sincerity. She turned to Lord Danning. "I believe it's time I returned home, my lord."

"Of course."

Suzanna bade goodbye to her friend and promised to meet up with her that evening. They walked to the carriage in silence. She stepped up into the curricle and settled her skirts.

No sooner had she done so than the carriage lurched to one side as Lord Danning stepped within. Immediately upon him seating himself, Suzanna was reminded of how little room the carriage sported. His broad shoulders left modest space between them. With a flick of the reins, they were off.

"You never answered my question, Suzanna."

She looked away from the shop fronts gracing Park Terrace and turned to Lord Danning. A frisson of desire shot through her at his intense gaze. She stared, captured by the longing in his eyes, before pulling her attention back to the road ahead. The feelings he evoked would not do at all. They were friends and nothing more. She swallowed. "What question was that, my lord?"

"If you would waltz with me tonight? I do mean to repair the damage I caused you last season, and I think stepping out with me this eve will ensure many a gentleman will ask for your hand."

He smiled, clasped her hand, and raised it to his lips. His eyes met hers just as his lips touched her glove and Suzanna reminded herself to close her mouth.

"I'm sure this drive today has more than helped, my lord. Besides, for all we know, it may have been something other than our disagreement last season that saw the *ton* term me a failure." Suzanna paused. "In any case, it does not signify what balls and parties to which society will invite me. I am determined to marry for love and to a man who is wealthy enough not to be in the least awed by my dowry. All I have to do is find him."

"Even so," he said, flicking the ribbons once more. "Will you waltz with me?"

"Yes, of course. I would be honoured." Suzanna looked toward her home looming before them, a haven she longed to step within before she became the blabbering fool from last season. Under the intense scrutiny of his lordship, it was only a matter of time before she blundered, and said something ridiculous.

It would be so easy to fall for his ardent charm and hooded, deep, ocean-blue eyes in which any woman would be willing to drown.

CHAPTER 8

The Moncroft ball was indeed a crush. People milled in every available space of which there was little in the undersized room. Suzanna and Victoria greeted the Countess and joined the throng. Few were recognizable due to the masks and dominos covering their faces and evening wear.

Suzanna looked about the ballroom in awe. Guests disguised in an array of masks—some plain and others decorated with gems—circulated and danced with carefree abandon. Beads, silk, and jewels sparkled in the candlelit room, giving the night an air of mystery and decadence.

Excitement thrummed in her blood. Never had she been to such an event. And as much as she wished to deny her feelings, Suzanna was excited about her forthcoming waltz with Lord Danning. To have his arms about her, pulling her close to his strong physique was enough to make this evening marvellous. Even unforgettable.

"It will be impossible to know to whom we are talking. I cannot even make out some of the women's hair colour under their wigs, not to mention their faces under the masks," Victoria said, looking about.

Suzanna clasped Victoria's arm and pulled her toward an area of the room that looked to afford more space. "Did Mr. Swinson tell you what he planned to wear this eve? He is to attend, I assume?"

"Yes," Victoria said, stopping a footman and taking two glasses of champagne. "But he did not tell me what mask he would wear."

"Do you like him, Victoria?" Suzanna asked. Not that she really wanted to hear the answer, should it be yes. Poor Henry would be devastated should he lose the affection of Victoria. But as her friend, she owed Victoria the opportunity to openly share her feelings.

"I do. Of course, I do. He is pleasant and always jovial." Victoria paused, a slight frown marring her brow. "He is certainly a favourite with Papa."

Suzanna nodded. "I should imagine so."

"Between you and me, Suzanna, I do believe Papa would like me to marry him. Not that I will, of course," she hastened to add. "But Mr. Swinson, for all his American ways, is actually the Earl of Manning's heir—a distant cousin, twice removed; but still the heir when all is told."

It was all Suzanna could do to hold the lump at bay in her throat over her friend's disclosure. Henry would lose this battle just as she lost the battle to stop being clumsy at the age of eighteen. Poor Henry, he would be devastated.

A lengthy silence settled between them; one Suzanna found difficult to breach.

Finally Victoria looked at her. "Should Mr. Swinson ask for my hand, the answer will be not to his liking or my father's, Suzanna."

Suzanna blinked and met her friend's gaze, the note of conviction in Victoria's voice leaving no room for doubt of her sincerity. "I cannot tell you how relieved I am to hear such news, even if it is at the expense of Mr. Swinson and your father's happiness." She clasped Victoria's hand. "Does this mean should Henry ask for your hand in marriage you would be in agreement? That one day will I not only be able to call you my friend but my sister?"

"Yes it does," Victoria replied, "if Henry should *ever* ask. Now talking of happiness, I do believe Lord Danning is heading our way."

All the air expelled from Suzanna's lungs when Lord Danning, dressed in a double-breasted coat with two tails stalked toward them, his heavy-lidded eyes fixed on one person.

Her…

Suzanna swallowed and then swallowed again when he towered before them. Tall and without a mask, his attention was obvious to any who cared to notice. Victoria, having such impeccable manners, politely bade good evening to his lordship, then walked away.

Unable to deny herself, Suzanna curtsied and took the opportunity to ogle his lordship's muscular legs, which filled his skin-tight breeches very well. The peculiar sensation of desire shot to her lower abdomen. No matter how much she tried to deny it, Suzanna was hopelessly attracted to him.

He leaned close. "You are the epitome of beauty this eve, Miss March." His whispered words sending a shiver of delight down her spine. "May I have this dance?"

Suzanna nodded, the ability to speak having vanished. His warm, gloved hand clasped hers, and he led them onto the floor. Other guests milled about them, readying themselves for the forthcoming waltz.

It took all Suzanna's will not to swoon when his lordship's arm settled about her waist. She caught the hint of sandalwood—an earthy, rich scent—as he pulled her against him. His chest was solid, his arms strong, yet his hands were gentle as they held her.

She cleared her throat. "I'm surprised you knew me, Lord Danning? My Egyptian costume fooled even my brother." She smiled in the hope it would mask her nerves. He was an excellent dancer, his steps sure and capable as they floated around the room.

"I would know you anywhere, Suzanna," he said, leaning devilishly close, the breath of his words tickling her ear. Suzanna turned and found her mouth deliciously close to his. Their gazes collided and locked. Time seemed to stop.

"I do not recall giving you leave to use my given name, my lord?"

"Ahh, but you did, remember? In the park yesterday," he said. "So may I, Suzanna? I promise to return the favour and allow you to call me Royce when we're in private."

Lord Danning's—Royce's—gaze settled on her lips. He was so close. So close, Suzanna had only to lean forward and their mouths would meet. Memories of his ardent, seductive kiss had her yearning for another. Another taste of sin.

A shrill laugh in the room brought them both to their senses. Lord Danning leaned back and smiled before settling them once again at a more appropriate distance.

"You make me forget I'm a gentleman, Suzanna." He sighed. "You do realize before this evening is over I'm going to thoroughly kiss you again."

Suzanna chuckled and raised her brow at the surety in his voice. "Really, *Royce*? And when, pray tell, will you have the opportunity to do so? I shall not be venturing to the terrace with you this evening, and you cannot kiss me here."

"I want to kiss you. Here and now."

Suzanna wanted it, too. Just the thought of engaging in such a naughty escapade before the uppity *ton* sent her rebellious side to sing. "Well you cannot. I forbid it." She smiled and allowed herself to relax and enjoy the dance. At times, their gazes would collide and the dizzying, wonderful roll in her belly would occur. But, like all good things, the dance came to an end.

Royce, the perfect gentleman, escorted her to a quiet corner within sight of the dowager countess and her aunt Agnes, and sought out a beverage for them both. Suzanna watched him retreat and cursed the coat tails on his suit that obstructed her view.

⚜

Royce watched Suzanna sip her mulled wine. Her lips, supple and red, kissed the glass rim, and his body tightened with need. Her unique emerald eyes took in the festivities before them, the slightest smile playing upon her lips.

He marvelled at the fact Suzanna had not the slightest conception of what a beauty she was. Last season, had he had more control of his temper, he could have proven his regard for her before she fled to Paris. Now with every word he spoke, Suzanna scrutinized, and wondered if he were being honest.

He knew she wondered when he would hurt her feelings again.

Yet he played no game, other than making her his wife. With every moment he spent in her presence Royce wished for more. He wanted her under his protection and his to hold for as long as time would give them. He wanted her to be the woman to bear his children and sleep beside him for the next fifty years, if they were so fortunate.

Royce took a calming breath. To demonstrate his love to Suzanna would prove difficult. His reputation as a rake, his past treatment, and his dislike of her brother were not obstructions easily overcome.

Nor was the fact he needed a wealthy bride and soon.

He paused. *Love?* Did he love her? He smiled when she laughed at something taking place on the ballroom floor. An ache settled in his chest that could only mean one thing. He did indeed love this woman. Wanted her with a need that at times scared and excited him, but also made him complete.

"Suzanna, if you're not already engaged, may I have the supper waltz?"

She looked at him in shock before blinking, and concealing her surprise. "Two waltzes in one night, my lord? You will create talk."

Royce took delight in her smile and wished he could always create such a reaction from her. "Let the *ton* talk; they are nothing to me, whereas you, Miss March are fast becoming everything."

"You flatter me, my lord."

"If you like," he said enjoying the rosy hue that settled on her cheeks. He stepped close and slipping his hand within the folds of her domino, clasped her hand. "I'll flatter and spoil you for all time if you'd only give me a second chance, Miss March."

Her hand was delicate and warm. His thumb slid over her silk glove, eliciting a tremor that ran directly into his heart. He noted her increased breathing and met her gaze. "Please follow me, and allow me to kiss you once this night."

"You are too bold, my lord." Suzanna took a sip of her wine and turned away.

"No amount of drink will calm your nerves, my dear. The attraction between us cannot be denied." He paused. "Please, Suzanna." He would beg should he have to. It was either that or throw her over his shoulder like a ruffian and carry her out of the room against her will.

She made an indelicate sound of protest and then nodded. Royce bowed and made his way toward the supper room doors. If memory served him correctly, a door within the room led to a passage that ran the length of the ballroom. At the supper room doors, he gazed over his shoulder and noted Suzanna following him at a discreet distance.

As he made the supper room threshold, he gazed over his shoulder and hesitated as Suzanna made her way toward him. Once she made the room, he motioned her to follow him into the passage beyond.

The air in the passage, cooler than in the ballroom, did nothing to dampen his desire to taste her again.

"I'm sure someone has seen our less-than-discreet disappearance, my lord."

"Royce. And you are well hidden under the mask and domino should they have noticed. Your escape into my waiting embrace will be our little secret, Suzanna." He pulled her into a darkened room. It smelt of cleaning oils and pine. Suzanna cautiously made her way forward then halted before a lady's writing desk. She turned toward him. Royce twisted the lock on the door, the snap of bolts loud as they slid into place. Suzanna eyed him warily. He stalked toward her and stopped when her hand settled on his chest.

"Royce, I should not be here embarking on such scandalous behaviour." She stepped past him, and he clasped her arm.

"Suzanna, I will not ruin you if that is your fear." He frowned and clasped her face with his hands. Her skin was soft, her hair smelled of jasmine. Unable to wait a moment longer to gaze upon her beauty, he untied the mask. The silk ribbon fell away from her chin, and Royce allowed the mask to fall on the desk behind her.

"I'm in love with you, Suzanna March. In truth, I do believe I fell in love with you the day I saw you in that ghastly frilly gown at your coming-out last season."

He smiled at her shock and kissed her. His body heated at her ardent response to his chaste embrace and the need within his soul roared.

Royce pulled back and waited for her to look at him. He enjoyed seeing her eyes cloudy with desire. "I wish for you to trust me, Suzanna. I have been termed a rake and a scoundrel, but I have never dallied with an innocent. I wish to marry you, honour you for all of our lives, and have children with you. Please give me a chance to prove myself worthy of your love."

"Oh, Royce." Suzanna swallowed the obscenely large lump wedged in her throat. Did he truly mean what he said? Did he speak the truth, or was he merely saying such things to have his way with her?

"I don't know what to say. I...."

"Say you'll marry me and make me the happiest man in London."

Royce kissed her again and Suzanna lost all line of thought. Heaven above, his kisses, no matter how quick, were enough to befuddle her senseless. And at this moment she truly needed to keep her wits about her.

"My brother does not approve of you and I do not know if I can trust you." As much as it pained her to see his disappointment, she truly did not. He had hurt her so last year when she thought they were forming a friendship. Henry kept terming him a fortune hunter. She prayed her brother was wrong.

"May I think over your proposal, my lord?"

He nodded. "Call me Royce in private please, Suzanna. And of course you may take your time. I'll not rush your decision."

Suzanna stilled when he met her gaze, and the heat that radiated from his eyes sent her skin to burn. "May the fine lady grant her humblest servant a kiss now?"

"I believe she will." When his lips touched hers Suzanna leaned into his warmth and nestled against his chest. His heart beat fast beneath the many folds of clothing, and oddly, Suzanna had the urge to remove them. To feel his skin, taste, and kiss him all over.

Heat bloomed on her face, and she was thankful Royce had his eyes closed. She was becoming scandalous with her wayward thoughts. Every time his lips sought hers and his hands touched her flesh, it left her longing for more, and strangely unsatisfied for something she could not name.

He pulled away and gazed at her. He ran his thumb against her cheeks, and the loss of his touch, his kiss, left a hollow feeling in her chest. Suzanna swallowed and couldn't form one reason against denying him further liberties, to allow herself to love him in the most intimate of ways a woman could love a man. He loved her, had asked for her hand in marriage. Should she say yes? No one needed ever to know they'd slept together before they wed.

It was a risk, on more than one level. She could become *enceinte*. Such a scandal would force her to marry a man her brother loathed. It was all very confusing and becoming more so with every kiss Royce bestowed beneath her ear.

The wooden side of the desk touched her legs as he moved her back. Suzanna, as if she weighed no more than a leaf, was lifted upon it. Paper scrunched under her bottom. She bit her lip when Royce's hand slid her silk gown above her knee. He stepped between her legs and for the first time in her life, the desire of a man lay against her own heated flesh.

His hardness did odd things to her body. She could not touch him enough. She wanted Royce to end the sweet ache between her thighs. She pulled him closer, wanting no space between them, and touched herself against his hardness. A sigh escaped as the contact went some way to dispel her need.

"We should stop before we cannot, Suzanna."

Royce's hunger-filled plea made her decision simple. She could not stop and did not want to miss lying with a man she loved and had loved all along, if she was truthful with herself. If she refused his offer of marriage, settled into a marriage of convenience with another gentleman and if by so doing she never again experienced this fire burning through her soul, her decision to stop would be forever regretted.

Suzanna refused to live with regret. She met his gaze and untied his cravat, hoping Royce did not notice her shaking fingers. He drew in a deep breath and Suzanna read in his pained visage his inner fight between desire and conscience.

"I think," she said, sliding his coat from his shoulders and revelling in the taut muscles beneath his shirt, "it is too late to stop."

Suzanna could not tell who undressed who more

quickly; she only knew there was no time to waste. The gown she wore was no impediment to Royce's competent hands, and was soon, along with her domino, tossed onto the already discarded clothing piled at his lordship's feet. The small room enfolded them in warmth and her skin shivered in sensual awakening.

Royce came against her and pulled her close. The hair on his chest was unlike anything she had ever felt before. It tickled and tempted at the same time. Suzanna licked her lips while her gaze devoured his upper body. Her fingers traced his chest and then moved to touch the muscles that descended like a ladder toward sin. A sin she fully intended to experience.

Suzanna murmured her delight when he laid her down upon the desk. He cupped her face and kissed her hard, his tongue demanding and tangling with her own. Suzanna welcomed his vigour and replied in turn as well as she could. Cool air caressed her silk-clad leg when he rucked her shift up to her waist. She rubbed her leg against his side and he growled.

She let her legs fall open and allowed him to settle between her thighs. Her skin burned, her body begging for something unknown but was soon to find out. Suzanna moaned when his hand cupped her most sensitive flesh and stroked.

Yes....

Royce was masterful at seduction, and without doubt, the rumours she had heard about town of his prowess as a lover were correct. Royce knew how to please a woman. He stroked her sex—soft, round movements tormenting her to madness. Suzanna opened her eyes when a low, seductive chuckle tickled her ear. She kissed him and allowed herself the delight of touching his back, the muscles flexing beneath his skin with his every movement.

"I must have you." Royce shoved his breeches down and Suzanna's mouth went dry. Never had she seen a man naked. Her lips curved. It was a marvellous sight to behold.

He came over her and she tensed as his manhood—hard, yet soft as velvet—pushed against her sex.

"I'll be as gentle as I can, my love."

Suzanna nodded and tried to relax. He eased into her; a strange and foreign pressure unlike anything she'd ever experienced. Then in one swift slide, he breached her maidenhead.

She gasped and swallowed a sob. A sharp pain tore through her sex and then settled to a light ache.

Within moments, the pain dissipated and where he now laid a new type of ache began—an ache similar to before but more powerful and urgent. Excitement over the unknown sensations Royce was eliciting tickled across her skin. Then he shifted his weight and moved, and comprehension dawned.

Suzanna's axis tilted.

Her hands slid to his buttocks and she squeezed. Sweat pooled upon his skin. She rubbed where her fingernails bit into his skin and kissed his neck and his chest.

"Marry me, Suzanna." Royce sought her lips and teased her with small beckoning kisses. "Please...."

To ask her at such a time was unfair, and yet all Suzanna could think was *yes*. How could a sane modern woman live without a husband like him? He was gentle, kind, and brought her body to life whenever he was present.

To walk away from such passion would surely be a mistake. Royce may not love her yet or more truthfully, she may not believe in his love at this very moment; but in time, with the sort of passion that sparked between them whenever they were together love was not impossible.

She gazed up at him, his sensual movements pushing her towards a cliff she couldn't climb fast enough. She saw hunger, passion, and fear in the window to his soul.

His fingers flexed against her bottom, and he rocked into her deep and hard. "Yes," she moaned. His movements threw her over an edge, and she fell into a void of utter bliss.

He allowed her to catch her breath before he asked, "Yes, you will marry me? Or yes, you're enjoying what we're doing on this desk?"

Suzanna smiled, but didn't reply to his teasing. Royce groaned and kissed the arch of her neck, sending tingles to race across her skin. He pushed within her, his body tensing, his own release as powerful as hers.

He untangled them and came to lie beside her, his hand cupping his head as he gazed at her. Suzanna clasped his cheek and ran her fingers against the short stubble on his jaw before letting her hand drop to her side. "I will marry you, Lord Danning."

His smile lit a spark within her soul extinguished twelve months ago. How strange life was. For months she had denied her feelings, kept them hidden under anger, and intentions of revenge.

But forgiveness and love trumped blame and hate. Soon she would be his wife. Lady Danning.

She grinned. The masquerade ball had been a magical evening indeed.

CHAPTER 9

Suzanna all but floated down the staircase in her brother's Mayfair home the following morning, unable to shift the smile from her lips. After making love with Royce, all her concerns and worries seemed to have vanished. He had asked for her hand and wished to marry her.

And she had said yes.

Suzanna hugged the wonder of it to herself and smiled at the footman who held open the breakfast room door. Thoughts of their forthcoming wedding day overran her mind. Since she had lain with him, the sooner they wed the better, just in case a little Lord Danning was already growing in her womb.

Love and longing filled her mind, and Suzanna couldn't wait to start the new life offered to her last night. After they had left the sanctuary of the small room, Royce had assured her he would call on her brother this morning to formally ask for her hand.

Suzanna frowned down at the eggs she was piling on her plate. Henry would react badly to the news. It was no secret he loathed Royce due to his previous treatment of her. But as she had seen fit to forgive it left her brother with no reason for ill will.

"Leave some for me. Have an appetite this morning, do you?" Henry came to stand beside her and looked over the sideboard.

Heat bloomed on Suzanna's cheeks, and she hastily added a slice of toast to her plate before sitting at the table. "Balls always leave me starved the morning after." Suzanna sipped her tea. "Do you have any plans this morning, Henry?"

Henry settled at the head of the table, and gave her a searching look. "I had a letter early this morning from Lord Danning. Seems he wants to meet with me at my earliest convenience. He should arrive at eleven."

Suzanna feigned surprise and nodded. "Do you know what about?" Butterflies took flight in her stomach at the thought.

"No. Not yet. But I'm sure I will soon enough." Henry cleared his throat. "Lord Danning has also asked for you to be present, Suzanna. Should I be worried about what is to be discussed in my library?"

Unable or perhaps unwilling to lie to her dearest brother, Suzanna shrugged lest she say anything that could throw her brother into an early temper. Such a reaction would be soon upon them once Royce formally asked for her hand, followed by her acceptance of such a request.

Silence settled between them like a cloak of doom. Henry was no fool and from the scowl upon his face, he appeared well aware of what was to come.

Suzanna steeled herself. It wasn't as if Henry was going to marry Royce and live with him. She was. So surely her brother would see past his own hatred of the man and let her be. Perhaps one day, even be happy for her.

She hoped.

❧

B y the time Royce arrived, Suzanna's nerves were frazzled and taut as a harp's string. Henry had chosen not to quiz her on the purpose of his lordship's visit, yet with a sinking feeling she knew there was no need. Her brother was no simpleton and no doubt had already worded his rejection of Lord Danning's suit to his sister.

At the sound of a knock on the library door, Suzanna turned. "Lord Danning to see you Mr. March," the butler said.

"Come forward, Lord Danning," Henry replied, his voice devoid of warmth.

Silently she watched as Royce moved across the room, and at Henry's curt gesture, seated himself beside her in front of Henry's desk. Dressed in a morning suit, Lord Danning had an air of elegance and ease. But his hands clasped tightly at his sides betrayed the disquiet running through him. Her heart tweaked a little knowing he wanted her enough to be nervous about the meeting.

Danning's wink and knowing smile nudged some of her apprehension away before her brother's brisk cold welcome brought her back to reality. Suzanna braced herself for the imminent question.

"You wished to see us, Lord Danning?" Henry gestured for him to begin and made a point of looking disinterested in the Viscount's presence.

"I've come here this morning, March, to formally ask for Suzanna's hand in marriage. A request I believe your sister is happy to receive and agree."

Henry nodded, his eyes as cold as ice chips. Without

moving his gaze from his lordship he asked, "Is this correct, Suzanna? You wish to marry Lord Danning?"

Suzanna looked at the two men she loved most in her life and wondered how she could make them allies instead of enemies, yet all the while she knew her next words would only increase her brother's animosity. "Yes. I wish to marry Lord Danning."

Suzanna met Royce's gaze and smiled. She blinked back tears from the overwhelming love blossoming in her chest as Royce clasped her fingers and kissed her hand.

Henry laughed. "I will not allow it. Frankly I'm surprised I allowed such a low-life cad as Lord Danning to enter our home. I will neither grant my blessing nor allow my sister to marry you, my lord. Now," Henry said, standing, "this interview is over. You may leave."

Suzanna frowned. "Henry, don't be so rude. I'm of age. Please do not make me marry Lord Danning without your approval. For I will. You know I will." She matched her brother's cold stare with one of her own.

"You will not, for I believe Lord Danning has not been as honest with you as he should. Would you care to enlighten my sister as to why you wish to marry her or should I?"

"Henry, I know not of what you speak but please stop this nonsense and be happy for me," Suzanna pleaded.

"Well, Danning?" Henry said, ignoring her.

"I love Suzanna; what more is there to say?" Royce smiled over to her but the light in his blue orbs had dimmed and dread clawed at her innards.

"Since you're unwilling to be truthful, allow me." Henry met her gaze. "I had hoped to spare you this pain, Suzanna. I truly did. I tried to warn you. But, I would never willingly hurt you and what I'm about to disclose I fear will hurt you immensely."

He threw down his quill. "It was one of the reasons why I welcomed your moving in a completely different set to Lord Danning and his calibre of friends for I hoped you would meet a man worthy of your heart. But," he sighed, "it seems my wish has not been granted."

"Say what you will, Henry," Suzanna said, all hope of her brother and Royce becoming friends fading to an impossible dream.

"At the beginning of last year's season, I attended a gambling den in the bowels of East London where I had the opportune delight, I would say, of playing Lord Danning's younger brother in a game of cards."

"Now what started out as a simple game of Piquet soon turned into a game of high stakes." Henry stood and marched to the window, his gaze on the street for a time. "I won, of course, George Durnham's inebriation and lack of concentration enabled me to win a sizable fortune from him. Of course, he signed a vowel, and I thought to receive payment in a week or two."

"I forgot all about the money he owed me until the night he started to spout off in Whites how he believed my sister had a tendre for his brother, and what a fool she was to think herself equal to such a match." Henry's eyes narrowed on Royce. "I should not have allowed the little fool to vex me, yet he did; and so I challenged him to a second game of cards. All or nothing. It was a challenge no gambling enthusiast could refuse."

Royce's hands clenched in his lap.

"I triumphed again over George Durnham. His lord-ship's brother wrote another vowel at my agreement. It was only when I received word of Lord Danning's cold and callous treatment of you that I demanded payment in full. For too long we've been shadows in the *ton* due to our family's heritage. The opportunity arose and I seized our revenge."

"Henry, what happened between me and Lord Danning was all a misunderstanding. Why do you continue to bring...?"

"Let me finish, Suzanna."

She remained silent and looked to Royce for support only to see him scowling at her brother.

"I demanded payment. Money I knew neither Lord Danning nor his brother had. For months I have been pulling the noose tighter about their necks. I am within my rights to obtain the money owed to me." Henry shrugged. "That the viscount's family has fallen on hard times is not my concern. But now as the head of the family and knowing Lord Danning wishes to marry my heiress sister, that," Henry said, striding back to the desk, and leaning over it, "concerns me greatly."

Suzanna was stunned into silence, not knowing how to react to such news. Her brother, for all his faults, was not normally a revengeful person. Yet after many months of snubs and exclusion from Lord Danning's set, perhaps her even-tempered brother had been pushed too far. As for Royce being out of funds, this was a shocking revelation. Not that she cared if he were poor, but more because he had hidden it from her.

An awful thought crawled into her mind. All the dances, the teasing remarks, and stolen kisses were an act and a way for Royce to make her fall in love with him so she'd marry him. And she had done exactly that—fallen for a man who was only after one thing.

Her wealth.

Suzanna met Lord Danning's gaze. "Are you penniless?"

He reached for her hand, and Suzanna pulled away.

He ran a hand through his hair and glared at her brother. "For years I have been trying to stop my brother from gambling and living a life of ill repute. But, alas, such actions were of no use. He continued to live a life well beyond his means."

"To keep the family name from being tarnished, I paid all the debts he accumulated. I continued to pay his bills and living expenses wherever they arose, here in England or on the continent. But the sum he owed your brother was too much. I could not pay it. I myself am to blame also. I have a tendency to love horseflesh, racing, and carriages. Not to mention my estate in Rome costs a fortune to upkeep while remaining empty for years on end. I admit I have not been wise with the Danning fortune."

"I've sold everything not entailed but it has barely dented the debt." Lord Danning sat forward in his chair and faced her. Suzanna looked at the floor, unable to look at him.

"I requested an extension from your brother, asking for time and received a curt and immovable refusal from his solicitor."

Suzanna looked at Henry and noted the hardened look of a man hell-bent on revenge. Bile rose in her throat.

"It is true, Suzanna," Lord Danning continued, "I was advised at the beginning of the season to marry an heiress. And it is exactly what I set out to do until I saw you back in London and looking as delightful as ever. I fell in love with you again." Lord Danning stood and lifted her chin to meet his gaze. "The night I shunned you was the night I found out my brother owed your brother a sum I knew I could not pay. I was in a temper and lashed out. You just happened to be the unfortunate person to encounter me at such an importune time. I apologized for my behaviour and ill humour before, and I will do so again. You did not deserve it."

Suzanna swallowed the lump in her throat and blinked back tears.

"Yet you still lie, Lord Danning. For months you have been gloating over the love my sister has held for you. Do not deny this. I imagine the idea of my own family's money paying off your debt to me filled your heart with selfish glee."

"Money and debt aside, you have never liked me, March, and out-manoeuvring you was not my aim. My financial situation did not change how I feel. I welcomed Suzanna's love and nothing in my past changes the fact I love her in return."

Suzanna looked from one to the other, not knowing whom to believe, nor wanting to listen to any more of this sordid story.

Time. She needed time to figure out what her heart and mind were warring about. Did Lord Danning love her or her money? That her brother would seek such revenge on any man was a sobering thought. This was certainly not the way they had been raised.

Time.

She took a deep breath and let it out slowly. But her heart still raced. "Lord Danning, in light of what has been said this day, I'm sorry but I cannot marry you."

Henry smiled. "I guess you should be leaving as it appears your business with our family is over, Lord Danning."

"Shut up, Henry," Suzanna snapped.

Lord Danning clasped her shoulders. "Don't do this, Suzanna. If you believe I would marry you only for your money we can have the marriage settlement signed over to you. In fact, shun your family's wealth and marry me as penniless as I am. But do not refuse to be my wife. I love you—only you and not your money."

Suzanna bit her lip, her mind a whir of thoughts. She shook her head. "I cannot. I need time to think. I'm sorry."

Without a backward glance, she fled the room. The despair on Lord Danning's face broke her heart. Yet was it the pain of losing her or a pain brought out by the fact he no longer stood to inherit her thousands of pounds?

That she could not answer.

CHAPTER 10

Months passed, and with it came the end of the 1811 season. Suzanna gratefully farewelled it and welcomed the fact she no longer had to attend parties and balls, pretending to be happy with her lot in life.

She was not.

In truth, she was terribly depressed and not at all sure she had made the correct decision with Lord Danning just twelve weeks ago.

Her brother continued to carry on as if nothing out of the ordinary had passed between them. It vexed her greatly. For all of Lord Danning's faults, he had made no fewer mistakes than her brother. Both, she'd decided, were as bad as the other. Revenge and tempers were two traits men should never combine; it only made for unhappy endings.

Her situation was a prime example.

Suzanna flopped onto the settee and sighed. Warmth from the fire warmed her skin, yet the unfulfilled desire to see Lord Danning again, to talk to him, left her cold and empty.

TAMARA GILL

Strange, but Lord Danning for the final weeks of the season had not been about in society. Suzanna had made quiet inquiries as to his whereabouts and was told he'd travelled abroad for the sale of one of his properties. Yet an inkling inside told her that this was an untruth and it gnawed at her conscience.

Where was he?

"Suzanna? Breakfast is ready. Are you not joining me?"

Suzanna looked up at her brother, noting the time. "I didn't hear the gong." She stood to join him. "Lost in thought, that is all." She walked to the door and paused on the threshold. "Henry, have you seen or heard from Lord Danning over the last few weeks?"

Her brother started and then shook his head while holding out his arm for her to take. "No. Why would I care what Lord Danning is about?"

His tone held a nervous, guilt-ridden tinge and all of Suzanna's fears surfaced.

"You know something. Where is he, Henry? I demand you tell me at once." Suzanna paused in the foyer and slid her hand from his arm. Her brother kept his face averted and refused to meet her gaze. What did he know?

"Where the blackguard deserves to be."

Suzanna stood, shocked, and watched her retreating brother's back before she collected her thoughts and ran after him, pulling him to a stop inside the breakfast room.

"Tell me what you set out to achieve has not come to fruition?" Suzanna braced herself for a truth she couldn't comprehend nor believe possible from a much-loved brother.

"Lord Danning is currently serving time in Marshalsea Prison. I suppose I should give the wretch credit for not fleeing England like his brother, doing the correct thing by his creditors, and paying for his crime. Of course, while he

84

is in prison, I'll never see the money rightfully owed to me by his sibling."

Had Suzanna not tried so very hard to convert herself into a lady these last few months, she could well box her brother about the ears at this very moment. As it was, it took all her control for her next words not to be shrieked like a banshee.

"Lord Danning is serving time...in prison. How could you, Henry?" Suzanna stormed from the room and yelled for the footman to have the coach brought around immediately.

Not one more second would she allow Royce to suffer the hell of living in a prison. Her mind whirred as to what her actions meant, but also, as a woman, how she could go about freeing his lordship.

She frowned then turned back to the breakfast room, annoyed further by her brother as he spooned large mouthfuls of ham into his unrepentant mouth.

"Get up. You're coming with me and you'll help me have Lord Danning freed. I know your desire to punish him has led to his current situation. You were raised as a gentleman, Henry. Father would be sorely disappointed in you, first, for gambling, and second, for being such an arse as to send a man to prison without a care."

Henry's fork clattered to the table. "I will not help you free him. Had it not been me, it would have been someone else who placed him in his current situation. Anyway, why should you care? I thought your infatuation with Lord Danning was over. Did you not play with him this last season, securing your own shallow revenge?" Henry sipped his coffee, brows raised mockingly. "I am not the only one who has succeeded in their game, it would seem."

Suzanna allowed guilt to swamp her. What Henry said was indeed true. She had allowed her temper to get the better of her. She had led Royce on a merry chase and tricked him into believing she welcomed his attentions when all along she wanted to cause him pain and humiliation.

But it had not been long before his charm, apology, and his constant attention toward her had broken away the stone that surrounded her heart and allowed it to beat once more. She had fallen in love with him again but only to turn her back on him when he needed her the most. For Royce to go to prison instead of jumping into a marriage with one of the multitude of heiresses gracing town proved beyond any doubts his love was true.

He loved her.

A smile quirked her lips. "I'm marrying Lord Danning, Henry. Today I will figure out a way to release his lordship and then I'm going to Gretna Green. Don't try and stop me or I will box you about the ears like I wish to."

Henry stood and threw down his napkin. "The hell you will, Suzanna. I forbid it."

With clenched teeth, Suzanna glared. "I doubt Victoria will be at all pleased the man she thought she knew and loved could act in such a callous manner. To first place a gentleman in debtor's prison—a gentleman, might I add, who Victoria counts as a friend—then to let him rot there without mentioning it to me is unpardonable especially when you are in a position to free him.

"Secondly, Victoria will not be at all pleased her best friend and closest confidante will end heartbroken because of an elder sibling who is too pigheaded to allow her to marry the man she loves. Perhaps I was wrong in voicing my approval of you to her, especially as Mr. Swinson has been chasing her skirts all season." Suzanna tapped her chin. "American he may be, but...perhaps he is a more suitable alliance for her family after all."

"Go," Henry said, his face turning a pasty shade of white at her threat. "In my desk you'll find the blunt to pay off the warden and free Lord Danning. It would be best, I think if you retired to Lord Danning's country estate until next season. I will ensure no word of you freeing Lord Danning reaches the matron's wagging tongues." A pained expression crossed Henry's face. "Damn it. I'm coming with you. If you're to marry the blackguard, let me give you respectability until you leave London."

"Sounds quite perfect," Suzanna said, smiling. "I do love you, Henry, never doubt my affections for you but you must let me lead my own life. And no matter what you think I will be happy."

Suzanna turned and marched toward the library, the snort of disbelief the only reply she received. Never mind; he would forgive her and eventually accept Lord Danning as family.

It may take some months or perhaps years, but it would occur. "Marshalsea Prison," she yelled out to the coachman a few minutes later, her pocket a great deal heavier with coin.

"Right you are, Miss March."

Suzanna smiled at the coachman's dubious look at her brother and wondered what other facial expression he could produce when she led Lord Danning out of the prison, and commanded him to Gretna.

It was certainly something to look forward to.

She chuckled.

CHAPTER 11

R oyce looked about the long, rectangular courtyard. The cold from the stone walls, starved of sunlight and allowed dampness to settle on his clothes. Clothes that after a month smelled more putrid than some of the inlets off the Thames.

He watched a woman collect water from the prison's only water supply, a hand pump in the middle of the court-yard, and sighed. His life was a disaster although no one at least could say he did not honour his debts.

It was some consolation that his stay here would be of a short duration. His steward had assured him only last week the crops were looking healthy and almost ready for harvest-ing. With the money due in from the sale of his private home in Rome, Henry March would be paid off, and his time in Marshalsea would be over. If only his investment in the East India Company and the Indiaman *Arniston* would dock safely and profitably, his stay would be even shorter.

The sound of the metal gates opening brought his attention toward the forecourt. Royce watched a turnkey escort a hooded figure into the prison—another poor soul unable to pay their way in society. He looked away and prayed the harvest would come soon and with it his release. Prison life, he'd found, did not suit his temperament nor standard of living at all.

"Lord Danning, you have a visitor."

Royce stood and the blood drained from his face. "Suzanna, what in God's name are you doing here? This is no place for a lady."

She looked like an angel, but some of the spark in her green orbs dimmed when she gazed upon the shoeless child playing around his mother's skirt. "I've come to apologize on behalf of my brother and myself. I was not told you were here."

He clasped her hand. Her soft skin mocked him over a lifestyle lost. Well, not for long. He had fallen low to be sure, but he was determined to pull himself out of this financial mess. "You have nothing to apologize for, Suzanna. My family's situation is my burden to bear."

"That may be so," she said, pulling him to sit beside her on the bench. "But I feel the actions of our brothers, mine in particular, have positioned you where you are this day. I am sorry for it."

Royce smiled and breathed in her clean scent. Suzanna smelled fresh, her skin porcelain white, yet her cheeks had a rosy hue from the cold yard in which they sat. "I do thank you for coming but you should leave. I would hate for you to catch a chill on my account."

"Lord Danning," she said, gazing at him in seriousness. "What you said that day in my brother's library about being in love with me. Was it true?"

Royce frowned. "Do not doubt me, Suzanna. Every word I spoke was true, *is* still true. I so love you and think of you often." She was his first thought in the morning and the last one at night.

Tears welled in her emerald orbs, and Royce had an overwhelming urge to comfort her. But he did not. The last thing Suzanna needed at this moment was a comforting hug from a man who reeked of the cesspit.

"I do not doubt you, Royce, and I'm glad to hear you were in earnest. Now," she said, standing, "come, gather whatever you wish to take. We have a carriage waiting."

Royce looked up at her and wondered for a moment if the love of his life had lost her wits since walking through the prison gates. "I cannot leave, Suzanna. I have debts still to pay and some months yet to serve. As much as I would love to flee with you, you must see 'tis not possible."

"Yes it is," she said, pulling her kid leather gloves back on, a twinkle of mischief in her gaze. "I've paid the turnkey a sizable sum, of which I'm sure he is informing the warden at this moment. Your debts with my brother no longer stand. So when you're ready you are free to go."

Royce watched Suzanna stroll off toward the exit and then quickly caught up to her determined strides. "I will not allow you to pay my debts and free me. That is not the way of a gentleman."

She nodded then surprised him by leaning forward and kissing him full on the lips. Heat stole through his body at the gesture and it took all of his control not to clasp her tight against him and cover her in all his grime.

"And I refuse to allow the man I love to rot in prison due to two brothers who should've known better. I know you are not entirely responsible for your family's debt. Our brothers are to blame, and I will not allow my future husband to sit in Marshalsea because of it. Must I wait months to wed you? Of course, if it would make you feel any better you may pay me back with interest." She quirked her lips and strolled off again.

How he loved her. A strong, determined little minx was his Suzanna, and she would marry him. Had said she loved him. Never before had he wanted to exclaim his joy in front of all and sundry. "So you will marry me, Miss March?" Royce yelled out.

"Of course," she said over her shoulder before stopping to wait for him. "But if you do not hurry up, Lord Danning, I may change my mind."

Royce laughed, caught up to Suzanna, and kissed her soundly. The sound of laughter and jibes from the other prisoners soon faded, replaced by the undeniable passion and love that sang between them.

He reluctantly pulled away and went to collect his meagre belongings before joining Suzanna at the gate. "We will go to your brother directly. I will demand he give us his blessings and we'll be married immediately."

"There's no need. I've already told Henry I'm going to marry you with or without his approval. And I'm not going home in any case. We're for Gretna. Henry, in fact, is headed home right at this moment and sending my maid to meet up with us along the way. Your valet will be with her when they arrive."

"Gretna?" Royce followed her to the enclosed carriage parked before the prison and handed his bag to the waiting coachman. "What are you up to, Suzanna?"

"Nothing too scandalous, I promise you. We're for Gretna, where you'll marry me with the help of a smithy and his anvil."

Royce helped Suzanna climb into the carriage and followed her, seating himself beside her on the squabs. "You're serious?"

"Yes. Very. Now, make yourself comfortable, we have

over three hundred miles to travel." She scrunched up her nose. "However, at the first opportunity we will find an inn for you to wash."

Royce laughed and clasped her hand, wondering if the rest of his life would be as full of surprise. He found himself in awe of the wondrous woman who sat beside him. Somehow he knew life would never be dull.

❦

I t took only a few days to reach Gretna. The Great North Road was one Suzanna never wished to travel again. Long and arduous, the journey seemed to take forever, especially when one was looking forward to reaching their destination and marrying the man one loved.

A very vexing man, she was starting to think. Not once while alone in the carriage had he tried to compromise his future bride. Kisses he bestowed and willingly; but as heated as they became, her future husband would pull away, sit her back in the squabs and talk of the countryside or his estate.

He was driving her insane.

They were due to arrive in Gretna within the hour, and hopefully be married forthwith. Excitement and butterflies rolled in her belly over the hours to come. From this night forward, there would no longer be separate bedchambers. Tonight. Finally. Royce would take her in his arms and make her truly his.

Suzanna gazed at his profile as he took in the outskirts of Gretna. From the days of travel, a heavy stubble had formed on his cheeks and jaw which left him so unlike the man he was in London. Usually meticulously attired according to the *ton's* standard, now he sat beside her, cravat undone and shirt creased from sitting too long in his bag.

It didn't detract from his good looks. If anything, the dark, dishevelled appearance suited him. Perhaps she would ask him to keep his unshaven form.

The carriage rocked to a halt. Suzanna looked out the window and spied a whitewashed, stone building with a thatch roof. Single story and basic in design, Suzanna absorbed the location where she would marry her viscount.

"We're here. Are you ready to be my wife?"

Suzanna leant toward Royce and pulled him close for a kiss. Having learned from him what one should do when kissing, she opened for him and deepened the embrace. Royce tensed then with a growl, followed suit and pushed her back against the squabs taking her lips in a fearsome way.

Fire coursed through her blood. Her hands clasped the hair at his nape. If his kisses were anything to go by, tonight would be more memorable than the last.

She sighed as he pulled away.

"What are you sighing about?" Royce met her gaze, his eyes burning with unsated lust.

"I was merely thinking tonight we'll be husband and wife and all that it entails."

He quirked his eyebrow and smiled. "Indeed we will."

Royce helped her alight from the carriage and ushered her into the smithy. Within minutes, he had procured the services of the blacksmith and witnesses for their union. The marriage took less than fifteen minutes. Suzanna and Royce spoke their vows and with the clang of the hammer and payment of a few guineas she became Lady Danning.

"I love you, wife."

"And I you, husband."

The next morning, Suzanna slumped against the multitude of pillows in her bed at a local inn. She looked about the room the innkeeper had explained was for newlyweds. Native flowers sat in a vase upon the windowsill. Two chairs faced the hearth, and the bed she now occupied was big enough for a king.

A smile quirked her lips and she shuffled under the covers. Last night had been marvellous. And to think she could sleep with Royce every night, for the rest of her life, seemed a dream come true. One would wish never to get out of bed.

A knock on the door sounded and Suzanna looked about for him. "Come in," she said, pulling the blankets higher on her person.

A maid carrying a tray entered and curtsied. "Morning, my lady. Lord Danning wished me to inform you he'll be back post-haste but wanted you to have a hearty breakfast."

The aromas of ham, eggs, and tea filled the room, and Suzanna's stomach grumbled.

"Thank you. Place it on the table before the fire if you please."

"Yes, my lady."

When the maid left, Suzanna wrapped her cloak about her shoulders and sat in the armchair before the hearth. She ate with zeal, the plain food tasting like a feast.

"Suzanna?"

She turned and smiled as Royce came into the room. "Good morning, husband."

He laughed and came and sat on the opposite chair to hers. "I wish to speak with you. Have you finished your repast?"

Suzanna placed down her napkin. "Yes, thank you. What is it you wish to say?"

Royce pulled from his coat pocket a folded missive.

"Is it from Henry? Has something happened?"

He waved her concerns away. "No. Nothing of that nature. What I wished to discuss is in relation to us."

He paused at her worried frown. "Go on," she said.

"Suzanna, as you know, my family is no longer flush with cash. George's gambling and our irresponsible lifestyle have brought the Durnhams to the brink of financial ruin."

"Yes." Suzanna nodded, not understanding why Royce would bring this up now. She was wealthy enough for both of them. He no longer had to worry about debts.

"Prior to my stay in Marshalsea, I had a marriage contract drawn up between us. I've sent a copy to London for your brother to approve and sign. This is your copy."

"What does it say?" Suzanna held her hand out for the paper clutched tightly in his hands. She unfolded it and read it as quickly as she could. "This wasn't necessary, Royce," she said meeting his gaze. "Why did you do this?"

"It was right for me to prove to you and your family that my love is for you only and not your wealth. This had to be done."

"I never doubted it, my love."

"And you never will. Your dowry is to remain your own to do with as you wish. I received word from my steward the week you arrived at Marshalsea that the home farms are doing well, and our crops look to be plentiful this year. The sale of my Rome property has finalized. All I need now are my investments in the East India Company to pay, and I should break even.

"I am determined to pay back what I owe your brother, along with other debts George has accumulated without

touching your money. If I wanted to marry for such secu-
rity, I could have asked any one of the chits flush with cash
looking for a titled husband. But I did not. Honour and
love would not allow me to."

Tears streamed down Suzanna's face. She was sure she
could not love someone as much as she loved Royce right
at this moment. She tore up the contract.

"What are you doing?" He leaped forward, but
Suzanna had already thrown the document into the fire.

"I do not need a piece of paper to remind me I have a
loving husband. I trust and believe your love is true. And
you forget, Royce, in my family, when it comes to my
dowry I have the choice as to how I spend it."

He kneeled before her and hugged her about the waist.
"And how do you intend doing so, my lady?"

Suzanna kissed him. "By ensuring our family is never
bothered with trivial debts again. By bestowing on your
brother an income, should he exceed it, will lead to his
spending time in Marshalsea instead of his brother. By
keeping a close eye on your horseflesh expenditure and
perhaps the hiring of a nanny would be a good idea."

Royce frowned. "We have no need for a nanny." He
paused. "Unless...."

"Unless I'm with a child?" Suzanna smiled at her
husband's shocked countenance.

"You're pregnant?" he asked.

Her hand clasped her stomach, the small round hardness low on her abdomen declaring it indeed was so. "Yes."

"But when?" he frowned. "Not last night."

"No," she laughed, "the night of the masquerade ball."

"Oh, Suzanna." Royce lifted her and kissed her
soundly.

Joy unlike any she'd ever known or thought to ever
have assailed her. She was in love and married to a

wonderful man who loved her in return. And now a child from this magnificent affection grew in her womb.

"I will strive to be the best husband and father in London. I promise you this."

Suzanna kissed him and wiped away his tears. "You already are."

Dear Reader,

Thank you for taking the time to read *A Marriage Made in Mayfair*! I hope you enjoyed the final book in my Scandalous London series.

I adore my readers, and I'm so thankful for your support with my books. If you're able, I would appreciate an honest review of *A Marriage Made in Mayfair*. As they say, feed an author, leave a review!

If you're interested in book one of my, League of Unweddable Gentlemen series, *Tempt Me, Your Grace*, please read on. I have included the prologue for your reading pleasure.

Tamara Gill

TEMPT ME, YOUR GRACE

LEAGUE OF UNWEDDABLE
GENTLEMEN, BOOK 1

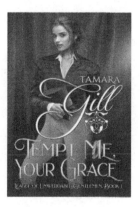

She was banished from England…and she banished him from her heart.

Upon her return to England following her father's death, Miss Ava Knight becomes the owner of one of the largest racehorse estates in the country. There's only one problem: the future of the estate requires a strong breeding program with the services of a stallion named, Titan. A shame that the horse is owned by a man she swore to never see again.

The Duke of Whitstone, Tate Wells, was heartbroken when Ava abandoned him on the night of their elopement, and he vowed to never lay eyes on Ava again. Despite Tate's unwillingness to forgive Ava, she comes to his aid during a deliberately lit fire at his estate. Someone is determined to destroy them. Now, the two are forced to work together to ensure the safety of their horses and their homes.

Will their previous feelings for each other rekindle their love, or will their feelings stall out at the starting gates?

PROLOGUE

Knight Stables, Berkshire, 1816

M iss Avelina Knight, Ava to those close to her, tightened the girth of her mount, and checked that the saddle wouldn't slip whilst hoisting herself onto one stirrup. With a single candle burning in the sconce on the stables' wall, she worked as quickly and as noiselessly as she could in the hopes that the stable hands that slept in the lofts above wouldn't wake.

Pleased that the saddle would hold, and that her mount was well watered before her departure, she walked Manny out of the stables as silently as possible, cringing when the horse's shod feet made a clip clop sound with each step.

Ava blew out the candle as she walked past it, and picking up her small bag, threw it over her horse's neck before hoisting herself up into the saddle. She sat there a minute, listening for any noise, or the possibility that someone was watching. Happy that everything remained quiet, she nudged her mount and started for the eastern gate.

There was still time and she didn't need to rush, now that she was on her way. Tate had said he'd meet her at their favorite tree at three in the morning, and it was only half past two.

She pushed Manny into a canter, winding her way through several horse yards that surrounded her home and past the gallop her father used to train their racing stock. Or what was once her home. From tonight onward, her life would finally begin. With Tate, she would travel the world, make love under the stars if they so wished, and not have to be slaves to either of their families' whims or Society and its strictures.

Tate and she would find a new life. A new beginning. Just the two of them until they expanded their family to add children in a few years.

Pleasure warmed her heart at the knowledge, and she couldn't stop the soft laugh of delight which escaped her.

In time, Ava hoped her father would forgive her, and maybe when they returned, happily married with children even, her father would be pleased.

The shadowy figure of a man stood beneath the tree. Yet from the stance and girth of the gentleman, it did not look like Tate. Coldness swept over her skin, and she narrowed her eyes, trying to make out who was waiting for her. Her stomach in knots, she pushed her horse forward unsure what this new development meant.

Ava looked about, but could see no one else. With a couple of more steps she gasped when she finally made out the ghostly form. Her father.

Her heart pounded a frantic beat. How was it he was here and not Tate? They had been so careful, so discreet. Why, they had not even circulated within the same social sphere to be heard whispering or planning. With Tate being the heir to his father, the Duke of Whitstone and

Ava only the daughter of a racehorse notable, their lives couldn't be more different.

Ava rode her horse up to the tree. She saw little point in turning back.

Pulling up before her father, she met his gaze, as much of it as she could make out under the moonlit night.

"Ava, climb down, I wish to speak to you."

His tone was not angry, but guarded, and the pit of her stomach lurched at the notion that something dreadful had happened to Tate. Had he been hurt? Why wasn't he here to meet her instead?

She jumped down, walking up to him, her mount following on her heels.

"Papa, what are you doing here?" she asked, needing to know and knowing there was little point in ignoring the fact that he'd found her out.

She dropped her horse's reins, and her mount reached down to nibble on the grass.

Her father's face took on a stern cast. "The Marquess of Cleremore will not be meeting you here, Ava. I received a note late last night notifying me that, as we speak, his lordship has been sent to London to catch the first boat out to New York. From what his father, the Duke of Whitstone, states, this was the marquess' decision. Tate confided in his father the predicament he'd found himself in with you, and that he didn't know how to untangle himself from having to marry a woman who was not his equal."

Ava stared at her father, unable to fathom what he was saying. Hollowness opened up in her chest and she clasped her shawl as if to halt its progress. Tate had left her? No, it couldn't be true. "But that doesn't make any sense, Papa. Tate loves me. He said so himself at this very spot." Surely she couldn't have been wrong about his affections. People did not declare such emotions unless they were true. She certainly had not.

She loved Tate. Ava thought back to all the times he'd taken liberties with her, kissing her, touching her, spending copious amounts of time with her and it had all been meaningless to him. She had been a mere distraction, a plaything for a man of his stature.

Her stomach roiled at the idea and she stumbled to the tree, clutching it for support. "No. I do not believe it. Tate wouldn't do that to me. He loves me as I love him and we're going to marry each other." Ava stared down at the ground for a moment, her mind reeling before she rounded on her father. "I need to see him. He needs to tell me this to my face."

"Lord Cleremore has already left for town. And by morning, he'll be on a ship to America." Her father sighed, coming over to her and taking her hand. "I thought your attachment to him was a passing folly. His lordship was never for you, my dear. We train and breed racehorses and, in England, people like us do not marry future dukes."

Ava stared at her father, not believing this was happening. She'd thought tonight would be the start of forever, but it was now the beginning of the end. Her eyes smarted and she was powerless to hold onto her composure. "But I love him," she whispered, her voice cracking.

Her father, a proud but humble man from even humbler beginnings, straightened his spine. "I know you think you did, but it wasn't love. You're young, too young to be throwing your life away on a boy who would have his way with you and then marry another titled, well-connected woman."

"I'm not ruined or touched, father. Please don't speak in such a way." She didn't want to imagine that Tate could treat her with so little respect, but what her father said was worth thinking over. The past few weeks with Tate had left very little room other than to plan, to plot. Would they have thought differently, would Tate have acted differently if he'd been older, more mature? If his departure showed anything, it was certainly that what her father was saying was true. He had regretted his choice and had left instead of facing her. Letting her down as a gentleman should, had not been his course. It showed how little he thought of her and the love she'd so ardently declared to him.

She swiped at her cheeks, wanting to scream into the night at the unfairness of it all.

"I'm sorry," she said, looking at her half boots and not able to meet his gaze. *How could he have done this to me?* She would never forgive him.

He sighed. "There is one more thing, my dear."

More! What else could there possibly be to say! "What, papa?" she asked, dread formed like a knot in her stomach at her father's ashen countenance. She'd seen a similar look from him when he'd come to tell her of her mother's passing and it was a visage she'd never wanted to see again. Ava clutched the tree harder.

"I'm sending you away to finishing school in France. I've enrolled you at Madame. Dufour's Refining School for Girls. It's located in southern France. It comes highly recommended and will help prepare you for what's to come in your life; namely, running Knight Stables, taking over from me when the time comes."

Finishing school! "You're sending me to France! But Papa, I don't need finishing school. You know that I'm more than capable of taking over the running of the stables already. And I know my manners, how to act in both upper- and lower-class society. Please do not send me away. I won't survive without you and our horses. Don't take that away from me, too." *Not when I've already lost the happiness of which I was so certain.*

He shushed her, pulling her into his arms. Ava shoved him away, pacing before him.

Her father held out his hand, trying to pacify her. "You'll thank me one day. Trust me when I tell you, this is a good thing for you, and I'll not be moved on my decision. We're leaving for Dover tomorrow and I, myself, will accompany you to ensure your safe arrival."

"What." She stopped pacing. "Father, please don't do this. I promise not to do such a silly, foolish thing again. You said yourself Tate was leaving. There is no reason to send me away as well." Just saying such a thing aloud hurt and Ava clutched her stomach. To have loved and lost Tate would be hard enough; nevertheless being sent away to a foreign country, alone and without any friends or support was too much to bear.

He came over to her, pulling her against him and kissing her hair. "This is a good opportunity for you, Ava. I have worked hard, saved, and invested to enable me to give you all that a titled child could receive. I want this for you. Lord Cleremore may not think that you're suitable for him, but we shall prove him wrong. Make me proud, use the education to better yourself, and come home. Promise me you will do so."

Ava slumped against him. Her father had never been flexible on things and once he'd made a decision it was final. There was no choice; she would have to do as he said. "I will go as I see there is little I can say to change your mind."

"That's my girl." He pulled back and whistled for her mount.

She couldn't even manage a half-smile as Manny trotted over to them.

"Let us go. I'm sure by the time we arrive back home breakfast will not be far away."

Using a nearby log, Ava hoisted herself up onto the saddle. The horse, as if knowing her way home, started ambling down the hill. Light shone in the eastern sky and glancing to her left, Ava watched the sun rise over her land. Observed the dawn of a new day, marking a new future even for her, one that did not include Tate, Marquess Cleremore and future Duke of Whitstone.

A lone tear slid down her cheek and she promised herself, there and then, never to cry over Tate again or any other man. She'd given him her heart and trust and he had callously broken them. That the tear drying on her cheek would be the last she ever afforded him.

And his precious dukedom that he loved so dearly. More dearly than her.

Want to read more? Purchase, Tempt Me, Your Grace today!

THE WAYWARD WOODVILLES
COMING SOON!

New spicy Regency romance series
Coming February 2022!
Pre-order your copy today!

SERIES BY TAMARA GILL

The Wayward Woodvilles

Royal House of Atharia

League of Unweddable Gentlemen

Kiss the Wallflower

Lords of London

To Marry a Rogue

A Time Traveler's Highland Love

A Stolen Season

Scandalous London

High Seas & High Stakes

Daughters Of The Gods

Stand Alone Books

Defiant Surrender

To Sin with Scandal

Outlaws

ABOUT THE AUTHOR

Tamara is an Australian author who grew up in an old mining town in country South Australia, where her love of history was founded. So much so, she made her darling husband travel to the UK for their honeymoon, where she dragged him from one historical monument and castle to another.

A mother of three, her two little gentlemen in the making, a future lady (she hopes) and a part-time job keep her busy in the real world, but whenever she gets a moment's peace she loves to write romance novels in an array of genres, including regency, medieval and time travel.

www.tamaragill.com
tamaragillauthor@gmail.com

Made in the USA
Monee, IL
04 October 2023

43977923R00070